RAP SUPERSTAR

DEBRA CLAYTON

Urban Books
6 Vanderbilt Parkway
Dix Hills, NY 11746

ISBN 0-7394-4901-X

Chapter 1

"Richmond, Virginia, where the hell are you?" twenty-four year old rap star, Animalistic yelled as he strutted across the stage. "If you're in the house, make some fucking noise!" His eyes scanned the massive crowd that filled the coliseum. Giant waves of bodies moved simultaneously to the music blasting from the huge speakers. The crowd roared.

"I can't hear you! If you're loving this shit, make some fucking noise!" He ran across the stage to another section of the audience. The crowd roared again. He walked over to the edge of the platform and looked down into the thousands of hands that frantically reached up for him.

This is the shit, he thought as a huge smile danced across his pretty-boy baby face. Although he collapsed into bed almost every night from exhaustion, the fans, the money, and the endless array of available pussy made it all worthwhile.

He ripped off his T-shirt and revealed the hard, ripped muscles of his chest and abs. His sweat-drenched body glistened. The crowd went crazy. He threw the shirt into the mob of fans chanting his name. Audience members dove over each other and fought to possess the coveted souvenir.

He hurried over to the left side of the stage. As he stood at the edge, he shouted, "Farmville, Virginia, where the fuck are you? Let me hear you make some noise!"

Screams filled the air. He laughed when a girl in the front row lifted up her T-shirt and exposed her breasts to him. This was nothing new. He would probably fuck her before the night was over if she was clever enough to get backstage. If she wasn't, another young lady would be the recipient of

1

savage lovemaking.

"Let's get fucking crazy!" He screamed into the microphone then walked over to a table, picked up a bottle of Evian water and guzzled it. He poured the rest over his body to cool himself down.

The music changed. Two scantily clad female dancers raced onto the stage and took their positions. The crowd went wild when they recognized the music of his current number one single. Right on cue, the dancers gyrated to the beat that pounded through the arena. He licked his lips and darted back and forth across the stage as he spit out the lyrics to his multi-platinum single.

> *And you and me, and me and you,*
> *Rolling on twenty-inch dubs,*
> *Hitting all the hottest clubs.*
> *You riding in my limousine,*
> *You checking my bling-bling.*
> *Your nigga likes to roam.*
> *Like McCauley, he left you home alone.*
> *Yeah, your nigga ain't shit.*
> *He's so fucking lazy.*
> *That's why I got your legs up in the air,*
> *Fucking you like crazy.*

He strutted over to one of his dancers and grabbed her from behind. Arrogance danced across his face as his hand slithered over her full, round breasts then crept down between her thick, man-eating thighs. He molded his body against hers as they gyrated to the nasty beat of the music. After he dragged his tongue up her neck, he bent her over, gave her three quick thrusts from his hips, then abandoned her as he raced back to the front of the stage. The men hooted and hollered while the women screamed.

> *I'm Animalistic,*
> *Don't go ballistic.*
> *Never seen a nigga rhyme,*
> *So damn futuristic.*

> *Niggas don't know,*
> *How I flow so sweet.*
> *Damn, spread your legs, baby.*
> *I think it's time to eat.*

The audience went crazy. He stood at the edge of the stage as his whole body bounced to the beat. His 6-foot 8-inch frame was drenched with sweat. His baggy jeans hung low on his waist, exposing his cotton boxers. Bursts of fire shot up from the stage and illuminated the dark arena. He continued to spit out lyrics as he gave his hyped fans what they wanted. He would be performing again for another sold-out crowd in two days.

Ten hours later, Animalistic rolled over in his bed. He looked at the naked woman asleep next to him. Her silky black curls spilled all over her pillow, and although he couldn't see her face, he remembered her. Carla, he thought as he recalled her name. She was a good fuck and gave good head too. She was a freak. He smiled as he thought about the night before. Some of things he had done to her were considered illegal in many states.

He glanced over at the clock. It was 6:00 in the morning. He didn't have time to hit it again. The bus would be pulling out for Greensboro, North Carolina in less than two hours. He reached over and gave one of her buttocks a quick squeeze before he slid out of bed. A nice, swollen ass was one of his biggest weaknesses; Carla had the kind that made a brother want to sleep in it all night.

He grabbed the empty condom wrappers off the nightstand and tossed them into the trash as he made his way to the bathroom. After a quick shower, he awakened the sleeping beauty. He thanked her for a good time, gave her a kiss on the forehead, and sent her on her way.

***

Twenty-one year old Randi glanced at her watch. It was 10:05 at night. She had another fifty-five minutes before she could leave work. It was a long night. Her feet ached from the black stiletto heels that she wore. Her tiny black leather skirt and white tuxedo shirt were not as neat and tucked in as they were three hours ago. Strands of her jet-black satin curls, once pinned up nicely, fell gently around her face. Her back ached from the large, round trays that she carried high above her head.

Although a few of the customers were extremely pleasant and the tips were more than respectable, the feeling of going nowhere fast plagued her. After working at Alexander Deveraux's, an upscale restaurant and bar, for the past two years, she had slowly begun to let go of her dream of becoming a writer. *A raisin in the sun,* she thought as she remembered the Langston Hughes' poem, "A Dream Deferred." Back in high school, it was just a reading assignment. Recently, the poem had become a painful reminder of her own shortcomings

Three years had passed since she had graduated high school with hopes of going to college and obtaining a career as a writer and filmmaker. Due to her family's economic situation, they couldn't afford to finance literary desires. Finances, along with the problems she had with her ex-fiancé, Eric, were enough to stall the pursuit of her dreams.

Eric was very controlling and overbearing. They had been high school sweethearts and he was her first and only lover. She had given herself to him completely, so when he had demanded that she forget about college and just be his wife, she succumbed to his wishes, and they were engaged. He gave her very little room for her friends and family, and she couldn't even look at another guy. Her family continuously warned her about him, but she was too consumed by him to listen. She convinced herself that the only reason he wanted to control her was because he loved her so much and didn't want to lose her. It wasn't until after she found out he was cheating on her that she saw him for what he really was. It was then that she tried to walk away from him. And it was that same night that he changed her life forever.

"It's not that bad," Mike, a co-worker said as he handed her the plate of food.

Realizing that she must have gone back to her dark place again, Randi quickly forced a smile as she grabbed the plate. "No, it's not," she said then hurried out of the kitchen to wait on more customers

As she buzzed around their tables, she did her best not to reveal her emptiness. She wore her pleasant but manufactured smile, which she kept readily available for days like this.

"Do you need any change?" she asked her customer as she picked up the money for the bill.

"No, sweetie," the elderly lady answered. "You keep the change. You have been an absolute pleasure."

"Thank you." Randi smiled. "You have a good evening."

"You too, darling."

Randi hurried back into the kitchen to turn in her money. Soon after, her best friend Kathy burst through the double doors.

"You're not going to believe this."

"What's wrong?" Randi was concerned. Maybe Mr. Allen had threatened to fire her again. Kathy was always getting into trouble at work.

"Guess who's here. You're never gonna guess who's here." Barely able to contain her excitement, she resembled a 3-year-old who had to go potty.

"Oh." Randi lost interest. "Who?" she asked dryly as she continued to count her money.

"No. Guess," Kathy insisted.

Randi sighed as she looked at her friend. Kathy was about to come undone. *Poor child*, Randi thought. Although Kathy got hysterical whenever a celebrity dropped by, Randi never paid them much attention. She wasn't gaga over Hollywood the way Kathy was. She thought the rich and famous were a bunch of spoiled brats who expected people to baby-sit their every need. She wasn't impressed with their status or their egos. She also knew that part of her resentment toward them was because they had achieved their dreams and she was just about to give up on hers.

"Kathy, I'm tired and I want to go home. I don't feel like guessing." She shifted her weight from one foot to the other in an attempt to relieve the throbbing pain.

"Come on," Kathy begged.

Randi sighed again. She knew that it was someone big by the way Kathy was acting. "Um . . ." She feigned interest.

"Animalistic!" Kathy blurted out. "Animalistic is here!"

Randi looked at her in disbelief. "Yeah, right. And of

all the fancy places he could have chosen to eat at, he somehow ended up here where I just happen to work." She was his biggest fan and Kathy knew this. Randi knew that Kathy was a notorious prankster, and this was just another opportunity to stick it to her. She wasn't going to fall for it this time. Although she gave Kathy's words no validity, she smiled inwardly as she turned and placed the money in the register. She wouldn't mind seeing his pretty bad-boy face tonight.

"Well, tonight's your lucky night, girl. He wants to meet you."

Randi laughed. "You know, I've got those papers on the Golden Gate Bridge if you're interested."

"No shit, Randi. He's really waiting to meet you," Kathy tried to convince her.

Bull, Randi said to herself, but decided to play along with Kathy's game. "Okay, Kathy, I'll bite. What does Animalistic, the future father of all my children, want with me?"

"Hell, I don't know, girl," she said as she grabbed Randi's arm and tried to pull her along. "But you sure as hell better not let him leave without meeting him." She tugged harder.

"All right, all right." Randi gave in as she pushed Kathy off of her. "I'll go, but you better not be playing with me."

"I promise you I'm not."

Randi narrowed her eyes as she stared at Kathy for another second or two. What if she was telling the truth? What if her future babies' daddy was out there waiting to meet her? Okay, she decided, being at the restaurant was believable, but him wanting to meet her was impossible.

"What the hell are you waiting on?" Kathy asked. "Come on." She grabbed her wrist and started pulling again. "You don't want to make him wait too long."

Randi followed as Kathy dragged her through the crowded restaurant. They navigated through the tables until they reached his.

At first glance, Randi couldn't see him because he was surrounded by his entourage and a group of autograph seekers. When one of his boys saw Randi and Kathy, he nudged Animalistic. He quickly looked up, made eye contact with Randi then turned his attention back to his fans.

"Oh my God," Randi whispered when she saw him. "It's him, it's him." She thought she might pass out. She looked at Kathy in disbelief. "It's him, Kathy, it's, it's—"

"See, I told you, girl. I wouldn't bullshit you over anything like this." She smiled excitedly

After signing a few more autographs, Animalistic rose to his feet. Randi looked up at him in amazement as he towered over them. When Kathy realized that her friend was in shock, she leaned over and whispered in her ear, "Breathe, Randi."

Randi nodded and repeated, "Breathe, Randi," never taking her eyes off the man of her dreams.

He smiled broadly, revealing all thirty-two of his perfect, professionally whitened teeth. He extended his hand. When Randi extended hers, he took it and brought it to his baby-soft lips. His eyes stayed on her face as they smiled mischievously down at her. "Animalistic." He introduced himself.

"I'm, um, I'm . . . " She tried to think of her name.

"You're Randi." Kathy assisted.

"Yeah, I'm Randi." Her voice cracked out of anxiousness. She cleared her throat and tried again. "Randi

Jacobs." She tried to remain calm, but inside she was doing cartwheels. She wanted to turn tail and run. How could she be meeting Mr. Animalistic while looking like a tired, run-down mess? She was embarrassed by her appearance.

He tried to make eye contact, but her shyness forced her to look away. This gave him the opportunity to size up the merchandise. His eyes roamed her body as they openly took inventory of her assets. One corner of his mouth curled into an approving smile.

"Randi Jacobs." He repeated her name. "You are fine as hell." He looked at her like she was the Last Supper and he hadn't eaten in days.

Randi forced a smile as she tried to ignore his roving eyes. "I'm a big fan of yours," she managed to get out.

"Really? I guess you'll be checking us out tomorrow night." He gestured for her to have a seat.

"I can't," she said to the invitation to sit down. She wished that she could because her legs were beginning to buckle.

"What about the show? You gonna be there?"

"I'm um, I'm working tomorrow night." She stumbled over her words. "I tried, I um, I had to work, I—"

"What time do you get off?" He looked at one his boys and gestured for paper and pen.

"Um, I . . . " She looked around nervously as if she was searching for someone who knew the answer to her question.

"Eleven," Kathy piped in and rescued her friend. "She gets off at eleven."

"Peep this. We're having a small party in my hotel room after the show. You could stop by and have a little fun."

"A party?" she asked as she tried to focus on what he was saying. Kathy nudged her excitedly.

9

"Let me give you the hotel name and the room number and I'll put your name on the list." One of his boys passed him the paper and pen. He scribbled the information and handed it to her. "You are gonna check us out, right?" he asked.

"Um, yeah." She nodded. Although she tried to relax, her body betrayed her. When she reached for the slip of paper, her hand was trembling.

Noticing that her friend was quietly losing it, Kathy stepped in and took the hotel information. "I'll hold onto this." She smiled then pretended to whisper, "I think she's in a little bit of shock right now."

"I see." He chuckled. "Can I count on you to make sure she stops by?"

"Oh, she'll be there." Kathy nodded confidently.

"Thanks."

"Oh shit," Kathy said as she grabbed Randi by the arm. "Here comes mister asshole. We've got to get back to work."

"I'll see you tomorrow night," he called after Randi as she was dragged away.

Randi stared back over her shoulder at him as Kathy pulled her. She couldn't believe she had just met her future babies' daddy.

His eyes followed her. He studied the way her hips swayed. She didn't posses the full, voluptuous ass and thighs of the women he was accustomed to fucking, but he was sure that she could handle him.

"Nice piece of ass," one of the guys from the entourage said.

Nice, he thought. *Very nice*. His smile broadened. He would be knee-deep in that tomorrow night.

Chapter 2

The next day, after she took care of her last customer, Randi anxiously rushed home to get ready for the party. She was still having a hard time believing that she had met Animalistic and that she was going to one of his parties. Kathy had to keep reassuring her that the previous night had actually happened.

After a quick shower, she slipped on the little black dressed she had picked out the night before. She stared at herself in the mirror and hoped that the dress wasn't too suggestive. It had taken her three hours to pick out that dress and now she was second-guessing it. She quickly slipped the dress off and began rummaging through her closet. She wanted to impress him, to make him say *damn* when he saw her. Now she wished that she had gone out and bought a new outfit for the night. After trying on a few more outfits, she ended up in the first one she had picked.

She nervously set her hair and applied her makeup. She had never been to an after-party before, and she wasn't sure what to expect. She had heard about some of the things that went on at parties like this one, but she was sure that they couldn't be as bad as they sounded. People had to be exaggerating about how raunchy they got. And even though wild parties weren't her scene, she couldn't give up this chance to hang out with an idol.

Randi knew that her mother would kill her if she found out she was going to a party like this one, much less hanging out with what her mother called a "gansta rapper." To make the situation worse, she was going alone. Kathy had made plans to be out of town for the weekend and couldn't go with her.

Once she was completely dressed and ready to go, Randi headed for the door. She reached for the doorknob then paused.

"I can't do this," she said, shaking her head. She stared down at her hand on the knob. "What if I'm just one of a hundred women that he invited to this thing? What if he doesn't even remember me?" She let go of the doorknob, turned around and leaned against the door. "What am I thinking?" she whispered. "I don't know him. I don't know anyone that's going to be at this party." She closed her eyes and she could see her mother scolding her. "Randi Lynette Jacobs, if you don't get in there and wash that crap off your face and take off that skimpy dress, I'm gonna skin your hide." Then she could see Kathy riding her. "Girlfriend, if you don't get your ass to that party and have hell of a good time, I'm gonna remind you every day of your life just how fucked up you are."

"Okay, okay, okay," Randi said as she opened her eyes. She turned around and grabbed the doorknob again. "Sorry, Mom," she apologized as she took a deep breath, opened the door and left for the party.

Within 30 minutes, she was at the hotel. She took a deep breath to calm her nerves as she stepped onto the elevator. It didn't work. Her heart pounded wildly as she rode up to the eighth floor. You can do this, she told herself.

When the doors opened, she stepped out of the elevator and noticed a group of people gathered in the hallway. Most were women. She hesitated as she wondered if all the women were there to meet Animalistic. Was she just one of many that he had invited? She bit her bottom lip as she contemplated running back into the elevator.

Then she thought about Animalistic, the way he

looked at her, the way he kissed her hand and smiled down at her. He was so perfect. And even though she didn't like men ogling her, Animalistic was different. He could do no wrong in her eyes. She had to do this. She would have to put away all of her shyness and inhibitions just for one night. He didn't even have to talk to her. Just being in the same room with him for a few minutes would satisfy her for the next ten years.

She began to walk down the hall to room 809 where the small mob congregated. The women made futile attempts to get into the room, but two security guards kept them at bay.

"What do I have to do to get in?" one of the women asked the guard as she pushed her body up against his.

He smiled at the other guard knowingly and responded. "What are you willing to do?"

"I'll show you my tits," the woman offered. She cupped her breasts through her flimsy, see-through blouse.

"I can see tits all day. What else you got?" he asked.

"Well, let's go around the corner and I'll show you what else I have to offer." She stroked his face with one of her scarlet red fingernails and pursed her matching red lips at him.

The first guard nudged the other with a silly grin on his face and asked, "You got this, man?"

"Sure, man. Go ahead." He gave him one of those *go and get her* slaps on the back. He would get the next one.The guard followed the woman down the hall and around the corner.

Randi had heard about women giving favors to the security guards just so they could see the performers, but she never expected to see it happen right there in front of her. Maybe this party was a little raunchier than she initially thought it would be. Her good girl sensibility told her to turn tail and go home, but the fan side of her told her that she'd better not leave until she had at least seen Animalistic. She

13

focused on the remaining guard as she managed to push her way through the crowd. After being shoved by a few angry fans, she reached the guard and nervously stepped up to him. "Um, uh, Animalistic invited me," she finally managed to get out.

"Yeah, you and every other chick here." He sounded as if he was already bored with her.

"Yeah, but um," she stumbled over her words, "he um, said he would um, put my name on a um, list."

"Yeah, yeah. What's your name?" he asked as he looked down at his clipboard.

"Randi Jacobs." Her heart pounded. What if she wasn't on the list? What if he had forgotten about her? She was sure he ran across hundreds of women. Surely, he wouldn't have remembered her. She started biting her bottom lip again as she waited for the guard. She prepared herself to hear "Sorry, but you can't get in."

He looked down the list of names on the paper he held. "Randi Jacobs," he repeated. "You're right. Your name is on the list. I guess you're his candy for tonight." He chuckled.

"What?" She grimaced at his statement.

"Never mind. You can go in."

"Aw, hell no!" one of the other women said. "My name's on that damn list too, and I've been waiting here for over an hour."

"Now, I've told you three times already that you're not getting in," the guard said.

"Well I've offered to hook you up."

"Honey, you ain't even fine enough to suck my dog's dick."

"Bitch!" the woman snarled at him.

"Take your simple ass home," he said as he opened the door for Randi to enter.

Randi tried to ignore the words between the security guard and the angry woman. She silently prayed that she would see Animalistic and he would remember her.

She took a deep breath as the door opened wider and loud music poured out of the room into the hallway. The thumping beat of 50 Cent's "In Da Club" made the room vibrate. She cautiously stepped inside, unsure what to expect. The door closed behind her. The aroma of pot filled the air. Half-naked bodies gyrated wildly to the beat of the music.

Randi was not a social butterfly, so she immediately looked for a safe haven to retreat to until she could work up the nerve to mingle. She saw a seat in a corner, quickly moved over to it and sat down.

The party resembled a giant orgy as bodies smashed up against each other, simulating sex acts. She could barely tell where one person ended and another one began. A few feet away, she noticed a group of people sitting on a couch passing a joint around. When they caught her spying on them, they held it up in her direction in an attempt to offer her a hit. She quickly shook her head and looked away.

Expensive alcoholic drinks fueled the outrageous guests. Women disappeared into the back rooms with two and three men at a time. One of the rappers who had performed earlier with Animalistic was with a woman over in a corner. The half-naked woman pushed her full, round behind up against his crotch. His hands gripped her rotating hips as he dry-humped her.

Where was Animalistic? She scanned the room for him. Her excitement about seeing him was slowly dwindling. She debated with herself whether she should stay or leave. He was the reason she was there. Although she was anxious to see him, the environment she was in made her very nervous.

While most young women her age enjoyed going out

and partying all night, she would have been satisfied curled up in front of the television watching movies or dreaming of seeing her own movies onscreen. She could either watch movies all day or spend hours in front of her computer pounding out stories and scripts that she hoped would make it to the big screen one day. Yes, writing was her passion, but hanging out with wild men and loose women was not her thing. Drinking and getting high was no desire of hers as well. She had seen how the influences of drugs and alcohol had strained her parents' marriage and her relationship with her father until he managed to break away from it.

She sighed as she thought about her father and his warnings to her about drugs and alcohol. He would be so disappointed in her right now. She clutched at her purse as she contemplated her next move. Either she could move around the room to find her future babies' daddy or she could head straight for the door to make her exit. Before she could make up her mind, one of the other rappers known as Cooney noticed her and stumbled over. She thought he was going to end up in her lap.

"Damn, baby girl, why you sitting over here all alone?" His speech was slurred. Before she could answer, he grabbed her hand and pulled her to her feet.

"Let me get a look at you," he said as he spun her around. "Damn, damn, damn, damn." He shook his head. "You make a nigga wanna fuck you and eat you at the same time." The stench of alcohol and pot seeped out of him and filled her nostrils.

Repulsed, she pulled away. She resisted the urge to slap him, but the look on her face revealed her anger.

"Hey, bitch, come here. Don't you know who the fuck I am?" He grabbed at her as he stumbled and almost fell. "I'm the m-man," he stuttered. "The man w-with the f-fucking

16

plan."

"Hey, hey, Cooney. What's up?" a familiar voice cut in. It was Animalistic. He walked toward them. "Leave the lady alone."

Randi was relieved to see him as she straightened her clothes and tried to gather her composure.

Cooney looked at Animalistic. "What's up, my nigga?" He grabbed Animalistic's hand and shook it. "This bitch don't know who the hell—who the fuck I am."

Randi kept quiet. She had seen her father drunk enough times to know that it was a waste of time to try to talk to someone in this condition. But she was sure that giving him a swift kick in his nuts would have made her feel a lot better.

"Calm down, Cooney," Animalistic said as he patted him on the back. "This is a guest of mines. She's here to see me."

"For real, man? No shit?"

"No shit."

"All right, all right. I-I'm sorry, man." He took one last long and degrading look at Randi. He wobbled. Randi felt naked as his eyes invaded her. "Well, you tear that ass up for old Cooney-Coooooon." He howled as he stumbled away.

So, he did remember her, she thought as she stared up at him.

Animalistic quickly apologized. "Forgive him. He's fucked up right now."

"Thank you," she said nervously. "He scared the crap out of me."

"He's harmless." He chuckled as he thought about her choice of words. He had never heard anyone over the age of fourteen use the word *crap*.

As he looked down at her, he hoped she wasn't as innocent as she sounded. Now it was his time to blatantly

17

undress her with his eyes. He flashed another thirty-two at her as he smiled approvingly. "Damn, baby, but you do look good."

Randi felt self-conscious. Maybe her dress was sexier than she initially thought. He finally took his eyes off her body long enough to look her in the face.

"You want a drink? We've got Cristal, Moet, beer."

"No, thank you. I don't drink."

"Really?" He was surprised.

"Long story," she said as if she read his mind. She smiled up at him. He was more beautiful than he was the day before. Her heart was pounding wildly again.

"I guess you don't get high either then?" he asked, his head cocked to the side.

"No."

"Good. Me neither." He was impressed. "But I do have to get my drink on," he said as he lifted his glass.

She smiled again. She felt shy.

"Well, Miss Randi Jacobs, what do you say we go in one of the back rooms?"

"For what?" He wasn't gonna try to sleep with her, was he? She wasn't that type of girl.

He knew what she was thinking. "C'mon. It's noisy as hell out here, and I'd like to hear every word you say," he explained. "We could have some privacy." He gave her a *you can trust me* smile.

"I, um . . . " She hesitated. Was she really gonna say no to him? "I—"

"C'mon." He reached for her hand. "I promise I won't bite." He smiled. "Not unless you want me to."

She laughed nervously. "Okay." She followed him as he led her through the bumping and grinding bodies to one of the empty bedrooms. Once inside, he closed the door and locked it.

"So we won't be disturbed," he explained when he saw the worried look on her face.

Randi watched him as he walked over to the bed, reached into his pocket and pulled out a colorful array of condoms. He tossed them on the bed then pulled off his shirt revealing his smooth, tight muscles. Without a word, he began unfastening his pants.

"Hey, wait a minute." Randi stopped him. "What are you doing?"

He looked over at her and smiled. "Getting ready to fuck you like you've never been fucked before."

Her mouth dropped open. "Are you serious?"

"Hell yeah. Now, take your clothes off, unless you just wanna suck my dick."

She became disillusioned by him that very moment. She had tried to ignore all the indications that he was a jerk, but she no longer could. He was a jerk. "I don't believe this," she mumbled as she shook her head. "I thought you were—"

"Believe it, baby. You're getting ready to fuck a superstar." He chuckled.

"I don't think so." She stared at him, feeling stupid. She knew he was no angel, but she didn't expect this.

"What's the problem? I'm gonna use protection."

"Protection." She shook her head again, looked up at the ceiling then back at him. "I'm sorry, but I'm not her."

"Her? Who's her?"

She smiled as she decided to forget about the fact that he was a rap superstar and instead focus on the fact that he was a full of himself jerk. "You know my mother raised me to be a lady, so I'm not going to get to raunchy with this, but I'm not the one who's gonna be sucking your dick tonight."

"What your momma raised you to be is frigid. Damn,

girl. Chill. Don't be so uptight, baby." He gave her a half-ass smile.

"Uptight? I don't even know you. Besides, your mother, if you have one, should have taught you how to act like a gentleman, even if you were raised by dogs."

"Roof-roof, baby," he barked at her. "Now c'mon, baby girl, let this dog give it to you like you never had it before."

Damn, this wasn't the same sweet-faced, could barely talk girl he met at the restaurant yesterday. She definitely didn't have a hard time finding her words tonight. He didn't mind, though. If she wanted to play hard to get, he could deal with that. If she wanted to put up a little fuss before dropping the panties, he could deal with that too. He knew it was all an act to make her feel better the next day. That way, she couldn't say she gave up the pussy too easy. It was all a game. He'd play along with her for a little while, but if he wasn't knee deep in her within the next twenty minutes, he'd have to pull another chick off the bench.

"Are you serious?" she asked. "Can you be for real?"

"Hell yeah. Now, come over here and get some of this." He reached for her.

She stepped away. "Not even," she said, placing her hand on her hip and narrowing her eyes. "You keep your hands off of me."

"You don't know what you're missing." He added, "Girl, I could fuck you so good that it would make your momma and grandma cum."

"That's nice. That's real nice." She didn't know whether to slap him for insulting her mother and grandmother or to laugh at him for such a weak line. Humility was obviously not his strongest feature, she thought as she turned and walked toward the door.

"Where you going?" He sounded surprised. Women never turned him down.

"I'm leaving. This isn't what I had in mind. I don't sleep with people I don't know."

"Do you know how many women would love to be in your position right now, how many women would love to fuck me just so they can go back and tell their friends about it?" Damn, he hadn't worked this hard since . . . Hell, he had never worked this hard. This bitch was acting like her pussy was made of gold. "I'm giving you the opportunity of a lifetime."

"While you're stroking your ego, why don't you reach down there and stroke yourself, because it ain't happening."

"Listen, if you don't want none of this, then I'm not gonna force you. I don't have to beg for it and I sure as hell don't jack my dick. I fall in pussy every day." He opened the door for her.

Fall in pussy every day, Randi thought. *Not mines.*

There was a girl dancing in the hallway. She looked in their direction when the door opened.

"It's just too easy for me to have to work for it. Besides, it's not like you got the only pussy in North Carolina. Pussy's everywhere," he continued. He looked at the girl then back at Randi. "Well, what do you know? More pussy." He smirked.

He looked at the girl. "Hey, ma. Come here." He held his hand out. She walked over to him and took it.

"You wanna fuck a superstar?"

"Only if it's you, daddy." She smiled.

"Well, tonight's your lucky night."

"No. Tonight's your lucky night. You just traded up." She slipped into the bedroom as she gave Randi a wicked smile.

"Just like that," Randi said.

21

"Just like that." He smiled. "You just missed out."

"No, baby." She smiled. "You just missed out. You are about to get into something that every man at this party has probably already been in."

"Fuck you, bitch!" the girl said to Randi.

"No, you're not fucking me, honey. You're fucking him." She grabbed the door and pulled it closed for them. Satisfied with herself, she held her head up high and left the party.

The next day, Animalistic sat on his tour bus as it pulled out of the hotel parking lot and turned onto High Point Road. He wore a small grin on his face as he thought about the night before. The smile wasn't for the girl he fucked but for the one that got away.

"Randi Jacobs," he said under his breath. He rolled her name off his tongue. Boy, she was feisty, he thought. She was fine as hell too. Evidently, she thought she was too fine to give up the pussy. He smiled at the way she handled him. His mouth played with a toothpick that he held between his teeth.

The bus pulled to a stop at a red light. He thought about the way Randi's hips swayed when she walked away from him. Did she intentionally tease him only to tell him no later? He thought about the way her dress clung to her body. Prick tease. He thought about her round face and her caramel skin. He remembered the way her big brown eyes narrowed when she informed him that she wasn't sleeping with him, and the way her red, pouty lips curled as she expressed no interest in him. He chuckled to himself.

"Randi Jacobs." He whispered her name again. "Miss Randi Jacobs from Greensboro, North Carolina. I could have shown you a good time. I guess you'll never know."

One of his boys sauntered up and sat down next to him. "That was some nice piece of ass you had up there last night. You know the one in that little black dress that Cooney was trying to get with. I saw you take her to the back. Was it as good as it looked?" He grinned.

"Don't know, man. Didn't hit it," he admitted.

"Didn't hit it? You pussy. Nigga, what's wrong with you? Tell me playa-playa ain't losing his touch." He looked at him in disbelief. If nobody else got the pussy, Animalistic did.

"Naw, man. Now, don't get me wrong. I got some pussy last night," he bragged, "but not hers. She was a quote-unquote good girl." He made quotation marks with his fingers.

His friend laughed. "All them hoes up in that piece, there were no good girls there last night."

"Oh, yes there was." He smiled and repeated to himself. *Oh, yes there was.*

"Oh yeah? Well, what in the hell was she doing up in there last night?"

"She was a fan," he said aloud. *But I thought she was just another piece of ass.*

Chapter 3

"Where my niggas at?" Animalistic bellowed out as he raced on to the stage of the Bi-Lo Center in Greenville, South Carolina. The sea of people roared as the number one rapper in the country emerged. Smiling at their response, he raced over to the left side of the stage and screamed, "Are my niggas in the house?" He stared out into the audience as he awaited their reply.

The men returned with a resounding "Hell yeah."

"I can't hear you!" he shouted as he put his hand to his ear. "Let me hear my niggas make some noise!" The men howled even louder.

He ran over to the right side of the stage and yelled, "Do my ladies run this muthafucka?"

The women screamed, "Hell yeah!" as they frantically jumped up and down and reached for him. This was one hell of a rush. He had no need for drugs. Performing was his drug of choice. His fans kept him high. He stood at the edge of the stage and shouted, "Let me hear you say the ladies run this muthafucka!"

"The ladies run this muthafucka!" they screamed back at him.

"Again!" he yelled.

"The ladies run this muthafucka!"

"Again!" he demanded as he leaned forward with a hand up to his ear.

"The ladies run this muthafucka!" they began to chant. "The ladies run this muthafucka!"

"Aw hell, no you don't!" He cut in. "The only thing y'all run is your damn mouths!" He laughed.

The men began to hoot in agreement while the women

24

started booing.

"Naw, naw, man. I'm just kidding y'all." He laughed. "You know I love my ladies. Without the ladies, niggas wouldn't know how to act."

The women began to scream and holler again.

"Now, for my ladies, just because I love you so much and I want you to be satisfied tonight, I'm gonna tell your niggas what they need to do when they get you home tonight." He ran to the center of the stage. "Now, fellas, can you hear me?" he yelled.

The men roared.

"Now, this is what you say to your lady tonight when you get her home." He looked at his DJ, gave him a quick nod, then looked back to his fans. After the music started booming through the arena, he sauntered around the edge of the stage as he bounced his head to the beat and began to freestyle.

> *You got a phat-ass booty,*
> *And a tiny-ass waist.*
> *Now, sit your sweet-ass pussy*
> *Down all over my face*

The women squealed with excitement as he licked his lips and continued.

> *Now ride my tongue, baby,*
> *And hold on to my knees.*
> *You grinding so deep, baby,*
> *a nigga can't even breathe.*
>
> *Now shake it, jiggle it.*
> *rattle it, then roll.*

25

Now, hold it still, girl
And feel how deep my tongue can go.

The women went into a screaming frenzy as he paused and squatted on the edge of the stage. He reached down and touched a few of their hands. They frantically pushed and shoved one another as they tried to get to him. So as not to start a stampede, he stood back up and continued his stroll around the stage.

"Now, to all my niggas. Now that I got all your ladies' panties nice and moist, I'm gonna help you brothas out. Once you've licked her and sucked her and tongue-fucked her, now that she's done creamed all over your face, this is what you say to her."

Now, drop to your knees
And return the favor.
Can I stroke your tonsils?
Deep-throat it, baby.

The men went crazy as they shouted out "Hell yeah!" in agreement.

"All right, all right." He laughed as he sprinted to the rear of the stage to grab a bottle of water. After guzzling it down, the music changed. His dancers raced onto the stage and took their positions.

Animalistic reemerged from the shadows and yelled into the mike, "All right, people. Let's get this muthafucking party started!"

Two hours later he shouted, "Greenville, South Carolina, I love you!" then disappeared into the darkness. The sounds of his roaring fans followed him as he hurriedly pushed his way backstage to get to his dressing room. *Another satisfied customer,* he said to himself as he moved down the hallway cluttered with people.

"Great job, Anthony," someone called out to him.

"Thanks," Animalistic responded without looking to see who it was.

"Damn, nigga, you did your thing," Cooney said as he slipped past him.

"Well, you know how we do, nigga." He laughed as he brought his elbow up to Cooney's chest.

"Ya know."

"You know your shit was tight too, nigga."

"Hell, I'm just trying to be like you, man." Cooney laughed.

"Practice makes perfect."

"You sick, nigga." Cooney chuckled.

"Yo, man, I'll holla at you later," Animalistic said as he started back down the hallway again.

"Holla."

He paused a couple more times to speak to people and sign a few autographs for fans who were working backstage.

"Yo, yo, Anthony," one of his security guards called out as he was passing by.

Animalistic stopped to see what he wanted. "Yo, man, what's up?"

"These young ladies have been waiting back here all night to meet you." He grinned as he gestured to the three scantily dressed females who stood anxiously next to him.

"Damn," Animalistic muttered when he saw the three beautiful girls. Barely wearing enough clothing to cover their tits and asses, he couldn't take his eyes off their nearly naked bodies. He sauntered up to the three beauties. They looked like they were ready to jump his bones. He licked his lips as he imagined what they would look like riding his dick all night.

"Hello," one of the girls said seductively as her eyes traveled over his glistening bare chest.

"Damn, baby. Y'all make my tongue hard," he said as he finally pulled his eyes away from their curvaceous bodies and looked up to their faces. "Triplets?" he asked when he realized that all three girls looked exactly alike.

"We're identical," one of the girls answered. "I'm Mia, and these are my sisters, Tia and Kia."

"Nice to meet you ladies." He grinned

"Hello," they replied.

"The pleasure's all ours," Kia said as she stepped up to him and placed her hand on his chest. She brought her lips to his ear and spoke softly. "I hope your tongue's not the only thing we make hard."

Before he could respond, he felt the tip of her tongue tracing over the edge of his ear. This gave him shivers. Damn, he was one lucky-ass nigga, he told himself. He grabbed a handful of her ass and pulled her closer. The smooth, round buttock in the palm of his hand made his dick hard. He pulled her hand from his chest and placed it on his crotch. She groped the thickness in his pants and marveled at the size.

"Damn, nigga, what you packing?"

Jealous that their sister was getting all the attention, Mia and Tia moved over to where the grab-fest was. Mia grabbed at his ass while Tia went for the crotch.

"You think you can you handle all three of us?" Mia asked as she nibbled on his earlobe.

"With what he's packing, we may not be enough for him," Tia responded as she gently squeezed the swollen bulge in his pants.

Animalistic grabbed another handful of ass and

squeezed. "Ladies, why don't you come by my suite tonight and I'll see if I can handle all three of you?" Tonight was going to be the ultimate. He wasn't gonna just fuck three beautiful women at one time; he was gonna fuck identical triplets. His niggas were gonna hate the hell out of him.

"That sounds like a plan," Mia said as she slid her hand across his six-pack and up to his chest. Tia purred as she brought her lips up to meet his in an attempt to kiss him.

He pulled away. "No, baby doll," he said. "No kissing, no kissing at all," he informed them. That was his one of his rules for the women he slept with. He didn't kiss them or eat them, and he didn't fuck them without a condom. He didn't know where they had been, and he wasn't gonna put his mouth on them or dip his dick in them without protection. While most of the women had no problem with his rules, a few tried to give him a hard time about them. Nevertheless, in the end, he always got his way.

"No problem, daddy," Tia replied. "Just fuck us right and we'll be happy."

Two hours later, Animalistic was hitting the three sisters like a freight train. His body glistened with sweat as he plowed into Mia doggie-style. She'd cry out every time he went deep. He'd back off a little then start pounding again. The other two sisters played with themselves or with each other as they waited for their turn to come around again. Sweat poured down his body as he worked on his fourth nut. His dick was sore, but it was still hard, and he wasn't gonna stop until it went down. He had never been so turned on before this night. Fucking three women at once gave him a hard-on that he couldn't get rid of. He felt like the Energizer bunny. He kept going and going and going. Mia finally announced that she could take no more so, he grabbed Kia and went to work on her again.

A few hours later, unable to sleep due to all the bodies crowding his space, Animalistic climbed out of his bed. Wearing nothing but his huge ego, he walked over to the window and looked out into the night. *Man, tonight was the shit*, he told himself as he looked back at the three naked women who still lay asleep in his bed.

Those girls were freaky as hell, and there was nothing they wouldn't do. He wasn't sure what he enjoyed more; fucking one of them in the ass or watching the other two eat each other out. Now they looked like three angels. Two hours earlier, they were trying to fuck his brains out—or was it the other way around? He wasn't sure, but he knew his dick was sore as hell. *Too much fucking,* he told himself. Damn, and he had to piss too. *This isn't going to be fun.*

A few minutes later, Animalistic was sitting in a chair watching the triplets sleep. Although this was the wildest thing he had ever done and he should have been pleased with himself, he was starting to feel like this was not such a big accomplishment anymore. What had he really done? He had just fucked three women who would have probably fucked any man that came along. They were hoes. Where was the challenge in that? Anybody could fuck a ho. He wanted a challenge, someone he could conquer.

Then he thought about the girl he met in Greensboro. Randi was her name. He was surprised that he still remembered it. He couldn't remember the name of the girl he fucked most nights, but he could remember Randi. She was the one who thought she was too cute to give up the pussy. Now *she* was a challenge. If he had fucked her, then he would have conquered something.

Then he thought about it longer. No, Randi was not the type of girl you try to conquer. She was the type of girl that you settle down with. She was the kind of girl you took home to meet the folks.

He thought about the way he treated her, the way he disrespected her, and the way he disrespected her mother and grandmother. She deserved better than that. He was surprised that she didn't slap the shit out of him for the way he had acted. He knew that his mother would have. He glanced over at the clock. It was nearly 6:00 a.m. He would be leaving to go back to L.A .in a couple of hours.

Chapter 4

Two weeks later, Animalistic maneuvered his black Lexus coupe through the unfamiliar streets of Greensboro, North Carolina. Struggling to follow the directions that Kathy had given him twenty minutes earlier, he asked himself why he was doing this. It had been four weeks since he had run into the young lady that he couldn't get out of his head. No matter how hard he tried to forget about her, Randi Jacobs kept easing back into his thoughts. Whenever he was with one of his many groupies, Randi Jacobs seemed to be there, watching him, judging him, making him feel empty afterwards. And no matter how great the sex was, how freaky the groupies were, he still felt dissatisfied.

Maybe it was the guilt that was eating him up inside. He felt like shit for the way he had treated her. He remembered the disappointed and disgusted look on her face when he revealed his true intentions to her. He remembered how her beautiful brown eyes lost their smile when she saw who he truly was. And now, a month later, the reflection of himself in her eyes was a disappointment to him.

Maybe, just maybe, he thought, if he could talk to her again, apologize for his actions, maybe he could get back to his life without her haunting him another second. Maybe if he could make those pretty brown eyes smile up at him again the way they did when she first met him, then he could get on with his life. He didn't know if it would work, but it was worth a try.

He glanced over at the bouquet of yellow roses that lay on the seat next to him. *Women like roses, don't they?* he asked himself. He hadn't done much apologizing to anyone, much less a woman. The only woman he had ever given flowers to was his mother. He hoped Randi liked flowers. He hoped she'd accept his apology and get out of his head.

***

Randi was exhausted. She finally had the night off and she wasn't about to do anything constructive. Donned in her favorite bunny-covered pajamas and a do-rag around her head, she looked more like an elderly woman than a 21-year-old. She didn't care. She wasn't trying to impress anyone. She was chilling with Martin Lawrence and Will Smith and they didn't mind her attire. She had paid her $3.50 at the local Blockbuster, and Martin and Will were hers for the entire evening. As she sat on her bed and painted her toenails, she watched the bad boys.

There was an unexpected knock on her door. After she paused the movie, she waddled up the hallway to answer it. Maybe it was her next-door neighbor who borrowed everything but never returned anything. Randi wondered what she wanted now. When she opened the door, she was completely taken aback. It wasn't her bothersome neighbor in her doorway; it was Animalistic accompanied by a beautiful bouquet of yellow roses.

He smiled when he saw her. As he surveyed her appearance, he realized that she hadn't expected company. Still, in bunny-covered pajamas, with a do-rag around her head and cotton stuck between her toes, she was beautiful. He couldn't deny that.

Randi opened her mouth but remained speechless. She was angry as well as stunned. What was he doing there? After the way he had treated at the after-party, he had some nerve to show up on her doorstep. Maybe he hadn't insulted her

33

enough, she thought. Maybe he was there to show her that he could be an even bigger jerk than before. She tried to speak again, but still her words abandoned her.

Noticing her loss for words, he decided to speak first. "You just open the door for anybody?"

Ignoring his question, she went straight for an explanation. "What are you doing here?" she asked, placing one hand on her hip like his mother used to do when she was preparing to hear some bullshit.

"I wanted to apologize," he started as he tried to hand her the roses. "These are for you." He hoped that she would accept them. All of a sudden, he was becoming nervous.

His *I'm the shit* attitude was starting to dwindle as he stared down at her *take no prisoners* expression. He hadn't accounted for nervousness. Who was she? She had no right to make him nervous. She had no right to judge him for his way of life. He was Animalistic. He was a rap superstar. Still, he had to admit that the way she looked up at him made him feel a little uncomfortable with the way he lived.

She looked down at the roses, then up at him. "Apology accepted," she said then closed the door in his face.

Okay, this isn't going to be that easy. He knocked again.

Randi stared at the door as she debated whether to open it again. Although she knew he was a jerk, he was still Animalistic. He was still one of the biggest rappers out there, and he was standing at her door with a bouquet of roses for her. She was both intrigued and put off by him. She bit her bottom lip as she contemplated opening the door again. After the incident at the after-party, she was sure that if she ever set eyes on him again, she wouldn't give him the time of day. But now . . . Now that he was at her door, now it was different. It was easier said than done.

He knocked again. She didn't respond. She just stared at the door, wondering what to do.

Animalistic stared down at the roses again. He had flown all the way from L.A. to apologize, and she wouldn't even open the door for him. He was getting impatient. Who the hell did she think she was? *Fuck that bitch,* he said to himself. He didn't need the aggravation. He was Animalistic, rap superstar. He didn't need to be begging for this chick's forgiveness. He threw the roses down at her door and started walking away.

Just as he was about to head down the steps, he stopped. *What am I doing?* He was pissed off because she hurt his ego again. That was what had got him in this mess in the first place, his big-ass ego. So what if she didn't throw the door open and welcome his apology with open arms? What had he expected? He had treated her like shit. He deserved much worse than a door closed in his face, he told himself. He decided to check his ego and give Randi the apology she deserved. If he didn't, he knew he wouldn't be able to get her off his back

Sucking it up, he turned around and walked back to the door. He picked up the roses, straightened them up, and knocked on the door again. "Randi, can you just hear me out?" he called out.

Randi stared at the door and started biting her nails. He remembered her name. It was a month later and he still remembered it. She was sure he ran across hundreds of women, yet somehow he remembered her. Why was he really there? What did he want from her? Why was he banging on her door?

"Please," he said. "Just give me ten minutes. I don't blame you for not wanting to talk to me, but I came all this way to apologize. Can you please just give me ten minutes of your time?"

Ten minutes, she thought. What harm could it do? It was just ten minutes. She'd listen to what he had to say and then he'd be on his way. After all, he did come all this way to say he was sorry. She opened the door and looked up at him.

Relieved, he smiled. "I'm sorry." He tried to give the roses again.

She ignored them. "What do you want from me?"

"I want to apologize."

"Well, you have." She stared up at his face. He didn't look as arrogant as he did a month ago. The mischief in his eyes was replaced with a serious, almost somber look.

"Well, I was hoping that I could talk to you."

"Ten minutes, right?"

"Ten minutes." He nodded.

Randi took a deep breath and stepped outside, closing the door behind her. She walked over to the railing and looked down at the parked cars. She saw a black Lexus coupe. She had never seen it before, and assumed that it must have been his. *Pretty modest for a rapper.* She thought he would have driven something a little flashier, like the rappers she had watched on *MTV Cribs.* So, he wasn't a showoff. That was nice, she thought.

He leaned on the railing next to her. "I just wanted to apologize for the way I treated you at the party." He looked over at her.

She didn't respond. She just continued looking out into the parking lot.

"I treated you like you were just a piece of ass and that was uncalled for. I should have been able to look at you and realize that you weren't like the other women at the party," he said in an attempt to explain his behavior.

"And how were the other women?" She already knew

the answer. She saw how they acted at the party.

"You know—loose, easy."

Some excuse, she thought. If he had come all the way to her doorstep to apologize, he should have come up with a better excuse than that one. "So, you're saying that if you had known that I wasn't easy, then you wouldn't have disrespected me?" She finally turned her head toward him and looked up at him.

"Yeah," he admitted.

"Maybe it's just the way I was raised, but shouldn't all women be respected?" She was sure that it had to be difficult for him to be a gentleman when he was surrounded by the type of women that had been at the party, but he didn't have to be so crude when she turned down his advances.

"Well, when I rehearsed it in the car on the way over here, it sounded smoother than it does now."

"You do have a mother, don't you?" She turned the rest of her body toward him. "Or are you just the result of an evil genius with a test tube and a mischievous plan?"

"Ouch," he said. He looked down at her. Five feet six inches was probably as high as she reached, but she had some gumption about her. "No, no evil genius here. I'm the product of a loving mother and father."

She couldn't tell.

"Your loving mother raised you to treat women like you do?" She knew she could have been nicer, but she didn't want to let him off that easy.

He smiled. "My mom would string me up if she saw how I treated women," he admitted. His mom would have also liked her.

"Women should be treated with respect, not like some hole for you to shove your dumb-stick in."

He chuckled at her choice of words, but agreed with

37

her. "True, but shouldn't these women respect themselves?"

She hesitated but then nodded. He was right. Women had to respect themselves if they wanted to be respected by others.

"Women throw themselves at me every day."

"You mean you fall into pussy every day." She knew her mother would have shoved a piece of soap down her throat if she heard her language.

"I'm sorry. I shouldn't have said that," he said.

"Why? That's what you do, right? Fall in pussy every day?"

He chuckled. Now his words were coming back to bite him in the ass. "You were at the party. You saw how the women acted. How can I show respect for a woman who's willing to give head to a security guard, a complete stranger, just so she can get in a room to sleep with me, another complete stranger?"

He made a good point, and it showed on her face. He smiled when he saw that she could appreciate his position.

"So, you treat women like crap because they lack self-respect, but why did you treat me the way you did when I told you I wasn't going to sleep with you? Did you enjoy insulting me?"

"No. I just thought you were playing hard to get," he admitted.

"So, I can say that's the reason you're here now. You think I'm playing hard to get and you like the challenge."

"No," he quickly said. "Not at all." He wanted to make sure she knew that wasn't the reason for his visit. "I just thought you deserved an apology. And because I was so rude to you, I thought the least I could do was deliver it in person."

That was nice, she thought as she looked away at the porch light. She watched as the moths and bugs congregated around it, and figured that he drew women to him the same way. They couldn't help themselves.

He walked over to the apartment building and squatted down, leaning against the wall with his knees bent. He laid the roses down next to him and rested his arms over his knees.

Could he be telling the truth? she wondered. Could he be sincere? She wasn't sure if she should be so quick to believe him. Nevertheless, he did seem like a different person. He didn't seem like the same person she met at the party.

She studied him. He was beautiful, she thought. The porch light revealed the smooth, hazel-brown skin of his face. It was flawless. His curly black hair was brushed up on top of his head. The tapered sides were trimmed short, but the top was longer. They started out as waves and ended up as curls. His lips were full, bow-shaped. He had a thin mustache that lay just above those perfect lips, traveled down the sides of his mouth and under his chin. Then there were those teeth; she couldn't forget those thirty-twos.

"You plan on staying for a while?" she asked when he got comfortable on the porch. She didn't like him getting too relaxed. Ten minutes wasn't that long. She got the feeling that he would try to squeeze a little more time out of her.

"Seems like you don't plan on letting me off the hook," he said.

"Why do I have to let you off the hook? You've apologized and I've accepted. What more do you want from me?" She looked at his hands. They were huge. He had a little bling-bling going on.

"Why don't you sit down?" he asked. He wasn't ready to leave.

"Why are you really here?" She was sure he had underlying motives.

He paused as he finally realized his true motives. It

wasn't the fact that he was trying to get her out of his head so he could move on with his outrageous lifestyle. It was the fact that he wanted her in his head. He had never met a woman like her and he wanted to find out more about her. He wanted to see what made her different. What was so special about her that she could say no to him? He sighed as he debated whether to tell her the truth about his reason for being there.

She waited.

"The truth is I can't get you out of my head. From the moment I saw you at the restaurant, I was like damn, that girl is fine as hell. I gotta get with her. And then you showed up at the party looking so damn perfect." He paused as he wondered if he should go on. He knew that if his boys could hear him now, they'd call him the pussy that he was acting like. But his boys weren't there, and they didn't know how he was feeling. If he was gonna say it, he might as well say it all. "When you shot me down at the party, that hurt, but my ego was too big to admit it. From that point, it seemed like you were haunting me and shit. I couldn't get you off my mind. I tried not thinking about you, but you're always there. I guess what I'm trying to say is that I like you and I want to get to know you better," he finally admitted. "I want to see what you're all about."

She stared at him. *He likes me?* That would be flattering if he was the guy she thought he was before she had become disillusioned at the party. Now he was just a guy who would do anything to get in her pants.

He waited for her response, but she gave none. She just watched him. "So, you're not going to say anything?" he asked. He hoped he hadn't just made an ass of himself by revealing what was going on inside him.

She hated that he was sitting there on her porch causing confusion in her life. A month ago, she thought this man could do no wrong. Yesterday, she still considered him the biggest jerk in the world. And today he was asking her to accept the fact that he liked her and wanted to get know her better. How could this one man cause so much chaos inside her head? "I don't get you," she finally responded. "I know you're a famous rapper and all. I was one of your biggest fans, but you can't treat me like crap one day and then say I like you the next. You can't drop by with roses and expect this to make it all better. I don't know what you want from me. I really don't. But if this is a nice, more civilized way to try to get me in your bed, it's still not going to happen."

She paused as she considered the fact that he had traveled all that way to apologize to her. It was more than she would expect out of anyone, especially him. She continued, "But if you are sincere in your apology, then I sincerely accept it. But that's as far as it goes." She was ready to go back inside now. This was too confusing for her to deal with. While part of her wanted to believe him, the other part of her wanted to guard her against any of his underlying intentions.

As she started walking back toward her door, he quickly stood up. "Randi."

She turned and looked up at him.

"I'm not trying to get in your pants." He hesitated then continued. "I was hoping we could go out sometime."

"Go out," she repeated softly, barely audible. "No, I don't think that would be a good idea."

He stepped closer to her, so close that he could see his reflection in her eyes. "And why not? I think I could learn a lot from you."

"But I don't think I could teach you anything."

"I'm sure you can." Their eyes connected. *So, this is how a good girl acts*, he thought. She was totally different from the women he ran into on a regular basis. He wondered if she knew how rare and special she was.

41

"So, what do you say? You be my teacher?"

He had a piece of lint on his silk shirt. She reached up and picked it off him while trying to ignore the smooth, brown skin of his exposed chest. He smelled delicious.

"Like I said, I'm sure I couldn't teach you anything." She slowly turned and started to walk away from him.

"Well, can I at least call you?"

"I don't think that would work either," she replied. "I've got to get back inside." She moved over to her front door.

He watched her. Although she said no, he didn't feel defeated. At least she wasn't slamming the door in his face. That was a big step in itself. He would give her some time to think about it, and he would try again.

He picked up the roses and handed them to her. "These are yours." His eyes twinkled. He felt a little more confident than before.

"Thanks." She took the flowers and smelled them as she looked up at him.

"Think about my proposition," he added.

She wasn't promising anything. "Good night." She opened her apartment door. She didn't know his true intentions, but she wasn't taking any chances. The draw to him was too strong, and she knew she could get herself in a whole lot of trouble fast if he wasn't on the up and up.

"Good night."

She left him standing outside.

Inside, she put the roses in a vase and arranged them neatly. Was he really interested in her? She wondered as she stared at the beautiful flowers. She carried them into her bedroom and set them on the TV stand. After she restarted the movie, she climbed into the bed and tried to get her mind off her visitor.

Her eyes traveled up to the roses. She sighed. She didn't know what to think about Animalistic. He had insulted her then traveled thousands of miles to say he was sorry. She knew she'd have to give him credit for that.

Her telephone rang. She rolled over and picked up the receiver. "Hello?"

"Hey." It was a man's voice.

"Who is this?" she asked.

"Anthony."

"Anthony who?"

"Anthony Talbert." He laughed. "Animalistic. I thought you were a big fan. You should know my real name," he teased.

She was a big fan, and she knew more than just his name. She knew his real name was Anthony Lamar Talbert, born November 21st, 1980 in Des Moines, Iowa. She knew that his favorite color was green, favorite food was Rib-eye steak and favorite sport was basketball. She also knew that he would rather have been a singer than a rapper, but he didn't feel that his voice was strong enough. What she didn't know was why he was pursuing her. "How'd you get my number?" She was curious.

"Your friend Kathy gave it to me when she gave me your address."

"Well, what is it that you want now?" He was persistent, she thought.

"Just wanted to say good night, that's all."

"Good night," she said.

"Hey, slow down. What's the hurry?"

"I thought you just wanted to say good night."

"I did, but you don't have to be in such a hurry to get me off the phone."

"I don't know what you want me to say."

43

"Tell me how I can get a date with you."

"You've got thousands of women who would give their right arm just to go out with you. Why are you interested in me?"

"Because you're different, and I want to get to know a nice girl. I've never met a woman like you before. You intrigue me."

"Before the party, I thought you were mister wonderful, but now I don't know who the real Anthony Talbert is. You don't respect women, and you don't even respect yourself."

"Respect myself? What do you mean?" Although he could admit that he hadn't always been on his best behavior when it came to women, he had never thought that he lacked self-respect.

"The way you treat women is not only disrespectful to them but to yourself as well. Have you ever thought about what these women really wanted from you? You think you're using them, but aren't they using you too? And don't you think you deserve better? Don't you think you deserve someone who is genuinely interested in you and not your status, your bling, your cheddar?"

He thought about her words. He used women and women used him. Hell, he knew he was fine, but he also knew that the sistahs he dealt with wouldn't give him a second look if he wasn't worth millions. Maybe she was right. Maybe he did deserve better. Maybe he deserved someone who *would* genuinely care about him and not his cheddar.

At twenty-four, he had slept with more women than he could remember. They didn't care about him, and he didn't care about them. He had blindly given himself to so many faceless strangers. Had he been so caught up in the whole rap game of fucking every beautiful woman who came along that he had lost his respect for himself?

"Are you still there?" she asked, interrupting his thoughts.

"Yeah. I was just thinking about what you said." He sounded different, and she noticed the change in his mood. She wondered if her words would truly have an affect on him. She hoped they would. No matter how bad he had treated her and countless other women, he was a gifted rapper and she felt that he deserved better than he had given himself. "Good. Now, can I get some sleep?"

"Oh yeah, sure. Can I call you again?"

She was confused about how she felt about him. She was torn between the person who knew better than to give into a womanizer and the person who still thought he was the finest thing that walked on Earth. She chose to go with her good sense. "It's probably better if you didn't call me anymore."

"Okay. I'll call you this week," he said before he hung up. He didn't want to give her a chance to respond. He smiled at the thought of her as he maneuvered his rental car through the streets of Greensboro to get back to his hotel. He would be heading to Atlanta for a show the next night.

Chapter 5

A few nights later, after performing at another sold-out show, Anthony sat in his hotel room in Charlotte, North Carolina. Perched on the edge of his bed, he watched as the blonde's mouth went up and down on his swollen manhood. Her sparkling blue eyes stared up at him as she nursed vigorously on his shaft. Placing one hand on the back of her head, he pushed her down, encouraging her to take more of him into her mouth. Without hesitation, she did. He moaned as he felt the tip of his penis slipping down into her throat.

"Damn, baby." He marveled at her skill as he leaned back and closed his eyes.

This was not how he had planned his evening. After his show, Poppi, Li'l Bit and Cooney had tried to convince him to hang out with them at the after-party, but he decided he would stay in. Randi had been on his mind and he wanted to give her a call to see if she had considered his invitation to go out sometime.

Upon returning to his room, he found Tammy, the beautiful blonde who was now sucking his dick, lying butt-naked and spread-eagle in his king-sized bed. His first thought was to fuck her good and hard, but then he thought about Randi. He remembered what she had said about him respecting himself, so he decided to ask Tammy to leave. But as he watched her lying there playing with herself, he decided that pussy was pussy and no self-respecting man was gonna turn down pussy from some fine-ass freak who was finger-fucking herself right there in front him. Minutes later, he had his dick shoved down her throat.

Realizing that he was about to cum, Anthony pushed

his hips up as he tried to drive himself deeper down her throat. He pressed harder on her head and began to moan louder. She nursed relentlessly.

"Suck it, baby. Suck my dick," he growled. "Oh shit!" He cried out as he came in her mouth. Without missing a stroke, she continued sucking until he was completely drained.

A few hours later, Anthony again sat on the edge of his bed. This time, he was not consumed by pleasure. This time, confusion had taken over. He pushed his hand through his hair as he thought about what he done a few hours earlier. He looked over at Tammy. She was still asleep. He thought about the sex with her. Even though it was wild and uninhibited, even though it was just the way he liked it, he still wasn't satisfied. *What do I want?* he asked himself. What was he looking for? Whatever it was, he definitely hadn't found it between her legs.

He sighed as his mind quickly slipped back to Randi. *She did this,* he said to himself. She was the culprit. She had infiltrated his life, and she was the one causing all of his confusion. Now he knew what she meant when she stood outside his bedroom door at the after-party and told him that it was his loss. She knew she had something special that he couldn't find in just anyone.

Until Randi, he thought that all women, with the exception of his mother and aunts, were whores. He thought the only thing they were good for was sucking his dick and fucking him any way he wanted. But then there was Randi. In his twenty-four years of living, after sleeping with countless strangers, he had never met anyone like her before, and he didn't think he ever would again. His occupation didn't leave much room for finding a nice girl like her. Running into her at Deveraux's was pure luck. She was a one of a kind, and he had to have her. He couldn't let her just walk away from him.

Debra Clayton

He stood up, slipped on his boxers, and glanced at the clock by the bed. It was 3:17 a.m. Although he had promised to call, he suddenly had an urge to see her. Greensboro was only a two-hour drive from Charlotte. If he left within the next few minutes, he could be there before 6:00 a.m. He wasn't sure how she would to respond to him just showing up on her doorstep again, but he didn't care. He needed to see her.

48

Chapter 6

Randi rolled over in bed and looked at the roses. They were in full bloom. She thought about Animalistic and smiled. Maybe with the right supervision he could be reformed. She laughed softly at the mere idea that he could change. She had a better chance of becoming the president of the United States, and she hated politics.

She glanced at her alarm clock. It was 7:58 in the morning. She rolled back over onto her back and stretched. Her thoughts remained on Animalistic. She hated to admit it, but she liked him. She liked the fact that he came all that way to apologize to her. Although she still questioned his motives, she had to admit that she was impressed by his attempt to smooth things over. She also had to admit that she was a bit disappointed when he hadn't called like he said he would. Although she told him not to, she hoped that he would. She wanted a sign from him that there was some truth in the things he said to her the other day. A call would have made him more believable.

Her telephone rang. She rolled over on her stomach and picked up the receiver.

"Hello," she managed through a yawn.

"Wake up, sleepy head," a male voice said. She recognized it.

"Animalistic?"

"Anthony. Call me Anthony," he answered. She could hear the smile in his voice.

"You weren't expecting me to call?"

"No, not really," she answered as she tried not to reveal the slight joy she was feeling because he had called.

49

"What are you doing?" he asked. He was happy to hear her voice again. He could also tell that she wasn't pissed anymore.

"Trying to sleep." He didn't need to know that she was thinking about him, she thought.

"Sleeping in on a beautiful day like this?"

"I don't know how beautiful it is, but I do know how early it is."

"Get up and go to your front door," he directed.

"Why?"

"Do you always ask so many questions? Just go," he teased.

She slipped out of bed, wondering what he was up to. "Okay, okay, I'm going to the door." She complied as she walked down the hallway to her living room. "I'm at the front door."

"Now open it."

She opened it. "It's open."

"Go outside and look in the parking lot."

She walked out onto the porch and looked over the railing. What was she looking for? She didn't see anything special, just cars. "Okay, I'm outside," she informed him.

"Are you looking in the parking lot?"

"Yes." Her eyes continued to scan the lot. They stopped when she saw the door of a cream-colored BMW open. She didn't recognize the car. A man stepped out talking on a cell phone. She did recognize him. It was Anthony.

"What are you doing here?" she asked, still on the telephone.

"See, there you go again with all the questions." He chuckled. She wore her pajamas with the bunnies again. He would have to get her some Victoria's Secret.

Randi tried not to smile as he walked toward the

building. She tried to fight it, but she couldn't deny that she was happy to see him again.

"So, what are you doing here?" she repeated into the telephone.

"I came to take you to breakfast." He walked up the stairs. "You do eat breakfast, don't you?"

"Yes, I do." *Don't you smile at him when he gets over here,* she told herself. He looked as fine as ever. She bit her bottom lip as he approached.

They both hung up their telephones.

"Good. I'm starving." He towered over her. She looked so tiny, maybe a size six. A size medium in Victoria's Secret would probably fit her.

She looked up at him and forced her face to remain expressionless. "And you're so sure that I'm going to have breakfast with you."

"No, but I'm hopeful."

"I guess I do have to eat." She studied his face and saw that mischievous sparkle in his eyes as they smiled down at her.

"Shall we?" He held his hand out toward her apartment.

"Come on in." She led him inside. "Have a seat. I'll be ready in a minute."

He didn't sit. He walked around and surveyed the living room. She stopped and watched him.

"Go ahead. I promise I won't steal anything," he teased as he paused just long enough for her to leave the room.

After she disappeared down the hallway, he resumed his snooping. First, he flipped through her CDs, checking out her assortment of music. Her collection included artists such as Montell Jordan, Maxwell, Jagged Edge, Joe, Boys II Men, and R. Kelly. She was into love songs. After he flipped through a few more CDs, he found all four of his on the bottom. He smiled. He assumed that he was also on the bottom of her list. He would work on that.

Next, he moved over to her bookcase. She was an avid reader. He was impressed. The only people he knew who read were his mother and his older brother. He looked over the titles. She had a lot of how-to books. Most of them were about writing novels and screenplays. Next to them she had a collection of fiction. Some of her favorite authors included Terry McMillan, Marcus Major, Michael Baisden and Eric Jerome Dickey and Carl Weber. He thought about her sitting alone each night reading. *She must get lonely*. He would work on that as well.

He wondered if she was single. He had assumed that she was. Maybe she had a man stashed away somewhere. He scanned the room for signs of a significant other. There were none. He smiled. Maybe she had room for him. Maybe she didn't want room for him. Maybe he didn't care. She intrigued him, and he wanted her. All he had to do was figure out how to make her want him.

He walked over to her computer. On the desk lay some typewritten papers. He felt a little devilish as he picked up a sheet and read. It was a poem. He chuckled at the title, "Chocolate Lollipop," and assumed that she must have one hell of a sweet tooth to write about candy. Soon after he began to read, he realized that candy wasn't the object of her fixation.

Long, tapered fingers,
Urging my body closer,
Tongue dancing across my belly,
Each stroke becoming bolder.

Rap Superstar

The flickering of its tip,
Uncensored and savagely wild,
You lick and suck and taste me,
I'm your lollipop; you're my child.

How many licks will it take,
Before my walls surrender?
Just how desperate is your tongue,
To taste my creamy center?

My trembling chocolate thighs,
Swollen, honey-dipped hips,
Caramel folds of womanhood,
Each aching for your kiss.

"Damn." He licked his lips and continued to read.

"Excuse me." Randi snatched the poem away from him. "That's private."

He looked down at her tiny frame. "I'm sorry. I didn't know."

Embarrassed, she picked up the remaining papers off her desk and tossed them into a drawer.

"I didn't mean to pry," he said when she turned around and faced him.

"I didn't mean to snatch them from you," she explained. "It's just they're personal, that's all." She didn't want him to see that side of her. She didn't want anyone to see it. Although she was shy, it was in her writing that she became uninhibited and free, that she could explore many worlds and personalities. She didn't have to be the boring Randi Jacobs who led a mediocre existence. Instead, she could make love to strangers, live in exquisite mansions, and foil the enemy's plans. In her writings, she could be the seductress who drove men mad or the villain who couldn't be captured or a powerful executive ruling a corporate empire. Her writings gave her power to say what she couldn't express in the real world, allowing her to take chances with her heart. Anthony had stumbled into a part of her world that she wasn't ready to share yet.

"Did you write it? He wondered if she had chocolate thighs, honey-dipped hips, and caramel folds of womanhood.

"Yes," she admitted. She was sure her face was crimson by now.

"That was tight as hell." He smiled. "I mean you've got skills, girl. You should be writing my rhymes."

"Thanks." She smiled back nervously.

"Does that smile mean you're gonna let me take you to breakfast?"

"Yes."

"Good. Now, where can we find something to eat at around here?"

"There's an IHOP down the street if you like that."

"Sounds good to me." They walked over to the front door. "I think I passed one on the way over here."

Minutes later, they were in traffic.

"Is this yours?" she asked as she watched him maneuver the car through the busy streets.

"No, it's a rental."

She turned and looked out the window. He glanced at her, hands folded in her lap and legs crossed at the ankles. She even sat like a lady.

"So, what are you doing down in Greensboro again?" she asked as she continued to stare out the window.

"We had a show in Charlotte."

"But this is Greensboro, not Charlotte."

"I had you on my mind, so I decided to drive down and see you."

She looked at him. "You drove down here to see me?" She was surprised and flattered.

"It was only a two-hour drive. I drove down last night after the show and got a room." He knew he was scoring brownie points.

She smiled inwardly. He had made two trips to see her in less than a week. Maybe this guy was sincere. Maybe he was on the up and up. She turned back to her window.

"So, you're a writer, huh?"

"I try."

"You in school?"

"Can't afford it."

Hearing the sadness in her voice, he glanced over at her. "You need some help?"

Surprised by his statement, she looked over at him. Was he offering to help her? She smiled at his kind gesture but felt that she couldn't accept it. "No, I think I'll be all right," she said. "But thanks for the offer."

"Well, it's no problem for me. I'd be willing to help you out. No strings attached."

"Again, thanks but no thanks," she said as she turned to look out the window again. Although she knew that he had more money than she dared dream about, it didn't diminish the magnitude of his offer. He barely knew her and he was willing to help her with school. She'd definitely have to give him credit for that.

"Well, if you change your mind, let me know."

She nodded as her mind wandered to her ex-fiancé, Eric. He hated her writing. He hated anything she did outside of loving him, and he did whatever he could to discourage her.

But Anthony knew about dreams. He had followed his, and he was a star because of his relentless pursuit of it. Now he was not only encouraging her not to give up on hers, but he was offering to help her finance them as well. That meant a lot coming from him, because he knew the struggle.

"So, what else do you write about besides getting ate out?" He looked over at her and wondered if she wrote from experience.

She blushed. " 'Chocolate Lollipop' isn't about getting ate out. It's about love."

"Love." He chuckled. "Yeah, about a woman who loves to get ate out."

"You're hopeless." She smiled.

"No, you're hopeless. Here I thought you were this sweet, innocent young lady, but in reality you are a closet freak," he joked.

"I'm still a lady." She was starting to relax.

He looked over at her. "I know you are."

Twenty minutes later, they entered the restaurant and waited to be seated. When the hostess approached them, she couldn't take her eyes off Anthony. Randi wasn't sure if it was because she recognized him or because he was so fine.

"Smoking or non-smoking?" the hostess asked as she studied his face.

"Baby?" He looked at Randi.

She shook her head.

"Non-smoking," he informed the hostess.

"Follow me."

He put his hand on the small of Randi's back as the hostess led them to their table.

They took their seats and the hostess handed them their menus.

"Don't I know you from somewhere?" the woman finally asked.

"No, I don't think so. I'm not from around here." He looked at Randi and smiled.

"Are you sure? You look—" Her mouth dropped open. "I know you. You're that rapper, Animalistic. My kids love you."

Anthony smiled. "That's me."

"Can I get your autograph for them?"

"Sure. What do you want me to sign?" he asked as he watched Randi and wondered what she was thinking. She wore no expression.

The hostess handed him a menu to sign.

"What's your kids' names?"

"Jessica and Corey."

He scribbled a message to the kids and signed his name.

"Thank you." She smiled. "My babies are going to hug my neck for this."

"Not a problem." After the hostess left, he looked at Randi. "Sorry about that."

"No problem. You just made two kids' day." She smiled but quickly looked down at her menu when he tried to make eye contact.

Seconds later, the waitress hurried over. She looked as if she needed a bib to catch her drool.

"Hello," she said in the sexiest voice she could find. She ignored Randi.

"Good morning." He looked up at her.

"Are you ready to order?" She stooped down beside him.

"You ready, baby?" he asked Randi.

"Yes." She ordered three eggs with pancakes, no meat.

He ordered the Breakfast Sampler. After the waitress wrote their order, she bent over to give him a full view of her large, round breasts.

"Do you see anything else that you'd like to have?" She smiled seductively.

Even after what she witnessed at the party, Randi still found it hard to believe that women acted this way toward a complete stranger.

Embarrassed by her disrespect for his date, Anthony gently took hold of the waitress's elbow. "I don't mean to be rude, but if you can't have a little more self-control, then maybe I need to speak with your manager about getting another server." His voice was stern but not angry.

The waitress stopped smiling and stood up. She looked down at Anthony. "Well, excuse me," she said, placing her had on her hip. She looked at Randi, rolled her eyes then walked off.

Randi was impressed with the way he handled the situation. Maybe he had been listening to her. Maybe he wasn't the same guy she met over a month ago. "You pissed her off," she said.

"She'll survive." He chuckled.

"You may have just lost a record sale."

"Maybe so, but I didn't drive up here to talk about her. I came here to talk about us."

"Us," she repeated. What was he talking about? There was no "us."

"Yeah, us. You, me, us."

The waitress returned with their drinks. He took a sip of his tea then continued. "You don't know this, but from the first time we met, you have done nothing but cause me confusion." He smiled as he reached for a packet of sugar and opened it.

"Me?" She laughed. "You're the one causing all the confusion. One minute you got me thinking you're the biggest jerk in the country and the next minute—" She paused.

"And the next?" He urged her to continue.

"And the next minute I'm second-guessing my opinion of you. Now you're acting more like the guy I wanted to meet," she admitted as she watched him add the sugar to his tea and stir it.

He chuckled. "Well, you can credit yourself for getting a brotha to change."

"Oh really? And why's that?" she asked after taking a sip of her water. She was happy to see that she had a positive influence on him. She hoped that he was sincere.

"Well, since I met you, jumping into bed with all these different women isn't as fulfilling as it once was."

"I'm sorry," she apologized. So, he was still a ho, she thought. Well, at least he was honest about it. She gave him points for that.

"Don't be." He tasted his tea again. "I've just realized that something's been missing from my life."

"Really, what?"

"A good woman to make me leave these hoes alone."

"Hoes?" She frowned at the term he used.

Realizing that he may have offended her, he quickly chose another word. "Women." He smiled apologetically.

She smiled back. At least he was trying.

"You see," he continued, "after our last conversation, I realized that you were right. I do deserve better. These chicks out here don't dig me for me. They try to get at me because I'm Animalistic. They don't know who the hell Anthony Lamar Talbert is, and they don't want to know. They're just there because of the fame. And I admit that was okay before. That is, until I met you. Those girls satisfied my ego, but they did nothing for my soul."

"Wow," she said. "Good for you." She was proud of
him for wanting more than just a warm body.

"Well, that brings me to my point."

"And what point is that?"

"Well, since I'm trying to be a respectable man, I'm
looking for a nice, respectable young lady to put on my arm."

"And?"

"And I wanted to see if you were interested in
accepting that role."

"You're not serious, are you?"

The waitress returned with their food. "Can I get you
anything else?" she asked. She was still smarting from
Anthony's last remark to her.

"No," they answered.

"And why not?" he asked after the waitress left.

"Because you're Animalistic. You're a big name
rapper. You could date anyone. Why would you want to see
someone like me?"

"Not someone *like* you. You," he said as he poured
ketchup on his eggs.

"But why me?"

"Because you're Randi Jacobs and I like you."

"But I'm a nobody. You could be dating Alicia Keys
or Ashanti or somebody like them."

After swallowing a mouthful of eggs, he responded.
"First of all, Alicia and Ashanti are cool peeps, but they're not
what I'm looking for. Second of all, and most important, you,
Randi Jacobs, are not a nobody. You're a future writer that's
gonna knock this world on its ass. You are also a self-
respecting, take no shit, beautiful woman that put this nigga in
his place. You are the first and only woman that has gotten
this brotha to stop and take a look at himself and the way he's

living. Besides that, I think you're cute as hell. Damn, girl, you make a nigga wish he could sing so he could serenade you and shit."

"Stop it." She blushed.

"So, what do you say?"

"Anthony," she managed when she finally stopped smiling. "I am flattered. Truly, I am, but I can't see you like that."

"And why not? You got a man?"

"No," she admitted.

"The niggas here must be crazy as hell."

"Why do you say that?" she asked as she took a bite of her pancakes.

"To let you run around here single."

"Oh." She smiled.

"So, why are you single? Why don't you have a man?"

Her smile slowly melted away as she pulled her eyes away from him and looked down at her plate.

He saw the change in her demeanor and wondered if he had opened a wound. "Hey, what's up? You okay?" He touched her hand.

She looked up at him as she thought about Eric. "I'm okay," she whispered, trying not to reveal her feelings.

Now he was really curious. He wanted to know what was causing the heartbroken look she wore on her face. "What is it?" he pried.

It had been a year since she had seen Eric, but the memories of what he did to her still brought her pain. They had met during their junior year in high school. He was an all-around jock. The guys envied him because he could pull the honeys, while all the girls fought to be the one on his arm. Although Randi thought he was a dream just like all the other girls, she was consumed with her writing and had little interest in dating. Eric, however, decided that Randi was the one girl he wanted to sport on his arm. They started dating and quickly became the envy of the school. Everyone thought they were the perfect couple.

If only they knew, Randi thought as she remembered the relationship. They started off as all normal couples do. He treated her very well, but shortly after she gave him her virginity, he became possessive. He started demanding that she spend all her free time with him. He wanted her to give up her friends and her dreams of going to college for him. When she refused, he grabbed her, slammed her up against the wall, and choked her until she gave in. She knew that she should have walked away then, but he promised that he would never hurt her again, so she stayed. A few days later, he dropped to his knees and asked her to marry him. Without hesitation, she accepted.

A year went by and Eric had kept his word. He never physically abused her again until one fateful night. That night, Randi received a call from a woman saying that she was pregnant by Eric. Devastated, she immediately confronted him. Without hesitation, he admitted that he had a baby on the way and that she'd better get ready to be a stepmother to it. It was then that she decided that she could do better. She told him that she was leaving him. Eric, however, refused to let her walk away so easily. After several futile attempts to get her to stay, he went mad. He began beating her, promising her that if he couldn't have her, then nobody would.

Randi swallowed hard as she remembered how close she came to dying that night.

"Hey," Anthony said as he squeezed her hand. He could tell by the expression on her face that she was no longer with him.

Realizing that she must have slipped away somewhere,

Randi quickly apologized. "I'm sorry."

"Talk to me," he whispered.

She slowly pulled her hand from underneath his. "I'm sorry. I can't." It was too painful to talk about, and too much to share with him so soon. She looked down at her partially eaten breakfast.

"He must have been some asshole," he said with a little attitude.

She looked back up at him and gave a slight smile to his remark. "Yeah, he was."

"Did he hit you?"

"Can we not talk about this?"

Anthony took her response as a yes to his question, *Coward*, he thought. Any man that would lay his hands on a woman was a coward. "Sure." He forced a smile. He wished he could track this guy down and beat the hell out of him, but Randi wanted to change the subject, so he let it go. "Now, let's get back to talking about you and me."

"There is no you and me."

"Not yet, but there will be." He winked.

She smiled at the thought of them dating. It had been over a year since she had seen anyone. The fear of getting into another relationship like the one she had with Eric paralyzed her. She didn't trust her judgment when it came to men, so she pretty much kept them at bay.

But Anthony was different. The idea of being his girl was flattering. Who wouldn't want to date him? But then she thought about his lifestyle. With all the traveling and all the groupies and all the temptations, how could a man like him be faithful to a woman like her? He had been with hundreds of experienced women, while she had only been with one man. She didn't know if she even knew how to please a regular man, and she definitely knew that she couldn't please a man like Anthony who had been with the best. She remembered when they were at the hotel and he asked her if she was gonna suck his dick. Although it was insulting when he said it, it was slightly funny now. He was expecting her to suck his dick, and she didn't even know how to give a blow-job. *Boy, he would have been disappointed,* she thought.

Anthony glanced at his watch. It was getting late and he had to get on the road. "Well, I gotta get going. I've got two hours to get back to the hotel before they take off."

Disappointed, Randi picked up her purse. "So, you're ready to go?"

"Not really, but I gotta. I can't miss the rest of my tour." He stood up. "You gonna get that?" he asked, referring to the check.

Randi looked up at him, but before she could respond, he laughed. "Just kidding."

He picked up the check, paid the bill and they left.

When they arrived at her apartment building, she looked over at him after he parked the car. The idea of being his girl was enticing, but also ridiculous. She knew she couldn't even consider it. With her issues with trust and his issues with women, they wouldn't make it past the first day. She'd be accusing him of cheating before the ink dried on their agreement. Still, she was flattered that a rap star—not just any rap star, but superstar Animalistic—had wanted to date her. This was one that she would have to tell her grandkids about one day. She smiled at the thought.

Anthony watched her smile. He wondered what she was thinking about. He hoped that she was considering his proposition. Their eyes met. He wanted to lean over and taste her soft smile. For the first time in years, he had found someone that he was willing to throw out all the rules for. His no kissing policy was voided when it came to Randi. Not only would he kiss her, he'd even eat the hell out of her. *Whoa, boy,* he told himself. He was way too far ahead of himself. Maybe he should wait until she agreed to a second date before he started picking a china pattern. He chuckled at his own thoughts. *China patterns, where in the hell did that come from?* They weren't getting married; he was just bucking for another date.

"I better let you go," she finally said.

"I guess I should be hitting the road. Stay right there." He jumped out of the car, hurried to her side, opened her door, and helped her out.

"And you said you didn't know how to treat a woman like a lady," she teased.

"You make me wanna be a better man." He closed the door and walked her to her apartment.

"Thank you for breakfast. It was nice." She looked up at him.

"Thank you," he said, "for obliging me." He kissed hand.

Those lips, Randi thought, were softer than they looked, and they looked featherbed soft.

"I do want to see you again, Randi," he informed her.

"That would be nice, but I told you—"

"Shhh," he whispered, placing his finger on her lips. "I'm not proposing marriage, just another date."

"We'll see."

He smiled down at her. "Yes, we will."

She turned to open the door and he stopped her. "May I?" He gestured for her keys. She handed them to him. He opened the door then gave them back to her.

"Thank you." She hesitated in the doorway.

Debra Clayton

"Good bye, Miss Randi Jacobs."

"Good bye, Anthony." She smiled.

He returned to his car. *You don't know it yet, Miss Jacobs, but you're gonna have a hard time getting rid of me.*

Chapter 7

When he got back to his hotel in Charlotte, the guys were already coming out and loading the bus. One of the other rappers known as Li'l Bit, saw him and came to meet him.

"Hey, dawg, where've you been?" Li'l Bit asked.

"I had some business to take care of."

They walked over to where the other guys were.

"Man, you missed a phat-ass party last night."

"Was it off the chain?"

"Hell yeah, man, and the pussy . . . The pussy was so damn fine it was ridiculous."

"Well, I didn't do too bad myself. Got back to my room last night and there was this chick waiting for me butt-ass naked," he said with a laugh.

"Nigga, you ain't even gotta go out looking for the pussy. The pussy just come to you."

"Well, you know it, nigga." He looked at his watch then walked over to the side of the bus and handed the driver his bags.

"I ain't mad at you, dawg," Li'l bit said with a laugh. "Now, check this out. These chicks were asking for you last night. I told them you'd be rolling down to Raleigh, so they gonna drive down to party with us tonight after the show."

"Good looking out."

"No problem."

Poppi walked over to them as they headed into the hotel so Anthony could return his car keys. Poppi was one of the older rappers. He was married and had two kids. While Anthony wanted to hide his feelings for Randi from the other guys, he felt it was safe to tell Poppi how she was getting under his skin. He knew Poppi wouldn't ride him for catching feelings for this girl.

"So, where were you this morning?" Poppi asked. "Did you go see that girl?"

"Yeah, man. I saw her," he admitted.

"Who? That ho you fucked last night?" Li'l Bit asked.

"What ho?" Poppi asked, a little confused.

"That nigga had some bitch waiting for him butt naked when he got back to his room last night."

"Randi?" Poppi asked.

"No, not Randi," Anthony answered.

"Did you fuck her?"

"Hell yeah, he fucked her. That nigga ain't married. He ain't got no muthafucking ring on his finger," Li'l Bit answered.

"Nigga, I ain't talking to you. I'm talking to Anthony. Did you fuck her?"

"Yo, man, don't jump on my back about this shit."

"I guess that means you did." Poppi looked at him with disappointment. "Nigga, you need help."

"Muthafucka, don't judge me. What am I supposed to do, give up pussy cold turkey for some chick?" Anthony asked as he tried to defend himself. "Like Li'l Bit said, I ain't got no muthafucking ring on my finger."

"Hell, I didn't know she was just some chick. I thought you were feeling this girl. I guess I was wrong. I guess she's just another piece of ass to you."

"Nigga, get outta my face. Go home to your muthafucking wife!"

"Don't worry, nigga, I will," he said as he walked off, shaking his head.

"Yo, Anthony, don't worry about that nigga." Li'l Bit laughed. "He so whipped that I could have sworn that I smelled his wife's pussy when he walked by."

"I'm not." He returned his keys to the girl at the front desk and she gave him a receipt. Who in the hell did Poppi think he was? Sure, he liked Randi. He liked her a lot, but was he supposed to stop living just because he liked her? They hadn't made a commitment to each other. Hell, he didn't even know how she felt about him. He made up his mind that until he knew that he and Randi had something solid, he was gonna continue to live it up.

Later that night, after the concert, Anthony and his boys sat in the VIP room of Club Afterthoughts. He quietly sipped on a glass of Cristal as he checked out the local talent. Only the finest women were allowed back in the VIP room. And from the looks of it, Raleigh, North Carolina, had no shortage of beautiful women. Perfectly applied makeup, not a hair out of place hairdos, professionally manicured fingers and toes, and the tightest, tiniest, most expensive outfits wrapped around young, taut bodies were the order of the day. He enjoyed watching his boys as they slapped, grabbed and groped perfectly shaped asses. The sistahs giggled nervously as they pretended not to be offended by the guys' roaming hands and vulgar language. *Anything to get with a baller,* Anthony thought.

He had seen this scene play out in front of him hundreds of times. The only difference now was that normally he would have been grabbing handfuls of tits and ass too. His original plans were to go out, get drunk and fuck some little honey all night long, but Poppi had ruined that for him.

He couldn't forget about the conversation they had earlier that morning. He remembered calling Randi "some chick." That was a mistake. Randi was more than just some chick, and he knew it. He knew why Poppi was giving him such a hard time. If he was gonna pursue Randi, then he had to do it right. He had to stop fucking every woman that cocked her legs open in front of him.

He knew it would be hard, but if Poppi could be happily married and still be in this business, then Anthony could at least try to control his hormones. He chuckled to himself as he thought about giving up all the pussy for a woman he wasn't sure was even feeling him. Caught up in his thoughts, he didn't notice the leggy beauty who had approached him.

"Hi, Animalistic," she said.

He looked at her. She wore a red form-fitting sequined mini-dress that revealed her perfect 36-26-36 figure. Her honey blonde hair tumbled down her bare shoulders, accenting her flawless, hazel-brown complexion. She was definitely the type of woman who could get him into trouble. He stood up and smiled. "Yeah, what's up?"

"I've been subtly trying to get your attention all night, but you appear to be immune to my charm." She smiled seductively.

"I'm sorry. My mind was somewhere else," he said as he sipped his drink and studied her full, inviting lips. He was sure she could suck a mean dick.

"I noticed, so I decided to try a more direct approach." Stepping closer to him, she placed her hand on his chest. "How about you buy me a drink and keep me company?"

"What's your name?"

"Misha Taylor." She smiled.

"I'll tell you what, Misha," he said, looking around for a waitress. When one looked his way, he signaled for her to come over.

She quickly responded. "Yes, sir."

"How about bringing another bottle of Cristal for Miss Misha Taylor?" he said.

The waitress nodded and hurried off.

"Cristal." Misha smiled. "My favorite."

"My pleasure," Anthony replied. "Do enjoy," he said as he set down his glass and sauntered away. He smiled as he thought about how easy it was to walk away. Maybe leaving all the women alone wasn't gonna be as hard as he initially thought. He was sure that a woman like Randi was worth the sacrifice. Suddenly, he felt the urge to call her.

To avoid causing a disturbance, he slipped out the back of the club and went back to his hotel room. Once inside his suite, he made himself a drink and debated whether to call her. He glanced at his watch. It was after midnight. Maybe she would still be up; maybe she was sound asleep. Either way, he had to talk to her.

After he put down his drink, he pulled out his cell and dialed her number. The telephone rang three times then the machine picked up. *Where the hell is she this time of night?* he asked himself as he waited for the beep.

"Hey, Randi, it's me, Anthony. I was just—"

"Hello," Randi said.

"Hey," he said again. "I was just leaving a message. I thought you weren't home."

"I just got in from work." She was surprised but happy to hear from him so soon. "So, what's going on?" She sat down on her couch, tucking one leg under her.

He walked over to the couch and sat down. "Just got in."

"So, did you make it back in time?"

"Yep." He smiled as he leaned back on the couch.

"No after-party?" She was curious.

"Actually, I went out for a little while, but I got to

71

thinking about you, so I left early."

"I hope thinking about me didn't ruin it for you."

"Naw, I wasn't really feeling the party anyway."

"You're not sick, are you?"

"No, not sick. I just needed to chill a little. Performing every night is stressful."

"I'm sure. So, when do you come off tour?"

"We've got two weeks to go."

Randi stood up and went into her bathroom. "Well, that's not too far away. Maybe you'll be able to get some rest."

"Hardly. Right after that I gotta go to New York to shoot a video for my new single."

She turned on the water in the bathtub. He could hear it.

"What are you doing?" he asked.

"Running my bath water."

"You want some company?" he teased as he pictured her naked in a hot tub of water. He licked his lips.

"Sure, come on in." She walked into her bedroom and sat on her bed.

"You wouldn't be saying that if I was right there." He chuckled.

"You're right. I wouldn't. There is something about you being over a hundred miles away that gives me a sense of security." She laughed.

He leaned forward on the couch. "Check this out. In two weeks, I'll be in New York shooting my video. How 'bout I fly down after the shoot? We could have a late date after you get off from work."

She smiled at the thought of him flying back down to see her again. "That would be nice."

"Is that a yes?"

"Yeah, why not?" She unbuttoned her blouse.

"What time should I pick you up?" He tried to hide his excitement.

"Ten o'clock. Is that okay?"

"Ten's great."

"Well, I better get off the telephone before my water turns cold." She slipped off her shoes.

"Okay, I'll let you go."

"Good night." She unfastened her skirt and let it fall to the floor.

"Good night." He hung up his cell and walked over to the bar. After he finished his drink, he went into his bedroom. He wanted to impress her. It couldn't be an ordinary date. He had to make that night special.

Randi slipped off her stockings, bra and panties then lowered herself into the hot bath water. It felt good against her skin. "Mr. Anthony Talbert," she whispered. He was coming back to see her again. She smiled. She couldn't wait to tell Kathy. She closed her eyes and slid deeper into the tub until the water rose up to her neck.

Chapter 8

The next morning while the fellas were boarding the tour bus, Anthony pulled Poppi to the side. "Yo, man, can I holla at you for a minute?" he asked.

Poppi handed the driver his bags and turned to look at Anthony. "Yeah, man. What's up?"

"Yo, man, I um . . . " He looked down at Poppi. "I wanted to apologize to you about yesterday."

Poppi smiled. "No problem, nigga. I was way out of line."

"No, man, you weren't. I know what you were trying to say, and I appreciate you trying to look out for a young brotha like me."

"No prob."

"Oh, and for the record, Randi's not just some chick. I like her, man. I like her a lot, and I really wanna see what can happen with her, you know?"

"Yeah, I know."

"So tell me, man. How do you do it? How do you stay faithful with all these hoes running around here chasing after us?"

"I just remember what I have at home. You know Cindy and the kids are all I got. I'm not willing to risk it for some chick who just wants to get fucked by a superstar."

"Is it always that easy for you, man?"

"Hell no. You see these chicks out here. Fine as hell and probably could fuck my brains out."

Anthony laughed. "They sure can."

"I get tempted, nigga, but when I think about some other nigga fucking Cindy, I say hell no. When I think about some other nigga living in my house and my kids calling him

74

Daddy, I say hell no. So, when those hoes try to get with me, I say hell no."

"Nigga, you crazy." Anthony chuckled.

"But seriously, man, if you get with Randi and she gets your heart, man, and then you start thinking about fucking up, you think about her being with somebody else, giving your loving to someone else. Then when these hoes try to get with you, you'll be able to say hell no too."

"That's some powerful shit, man."

"Hey, pussy is a powerful thing, but love is more powerful. When you fall in love, you'll know what I'm talking about."

"Thanks, man."

"So, you think Randi is the one for you?"

"I don't know, man, but I'll tell you what." He paused. "I can't get her outta my damn head."

"That's the way it's supposed to be, nigga." Poppi laughed.

Later that week, Randi and Kathy met at the mall so Randi could buy a new outfit for her date with Anthony.

"How about this one?" Kathy asked as she held up a red strapless mini-dress.

Randi frowned. "That's too suggestive."

"Oh really? And what does it suggest?"

"It suggests that he jump my bones."

"And that's a problem because . . . "

"I don't want him jumping my bones."

"Why the hell not? Lord knows you could use some dick by now. You haven't had a good fuck since—" She stopped herself.

"Since when?" Randi asked with a hurt look in her

eyes. "Since Eric raped me."

"Randi, I'm sorry," Kathy quickly apologized. "I didn't mean that. Baby, you know I didn't mean that."

"Maybe you're right."

"No, no I'm not. I'm stupid, stupid, stupid. Forget everything I just said and listen to me now. What Eric did to you was fucked up, but that was over a year ago, baby. You don't deserve to be locked up. He does."

"I just can't do this."

"Yes, you can, baby. Anthony seems like a great guy. He offered to help with school. He wants to support your dream. He's nothing like Eric."

"I know, but—"

"No buts. Anthony obviously wants to be with you, and you've been loving him from so far away. Now it's your time to love him up close. Don't let Eric fuck this up for you. You hear me?"

"It's not just about the rape, Kathy. I gave up everything for him. My friends and family, my dreams, and then I find out he's having a baby with someone else. After that, how could I trust somebody like Anthony, who lives so far away, surrounded by beautiful women all the time? How do I trust somebody like that? And what about the fact that I haven't been with anyone since the rape? What if we do make it to that level and he wants to make love to me? What if I can't?"

"I know you're scared, baby, but you just have to take it slow. Take your time and take it slow. And if you do make it to that level and you're still scared, then tell him. Tell him what you've been through, and if he really cares for you, he'll understand and you two can get help. There are things that you can do to get through this. Just stop running so damn much, okay?"

Randi nodded.

"Good. Now that we got the inside straight, let's work on the outside." She reached over and picked up a cream-colored suit. "How about this? It doesn't say *jump my bones*. It says *I'm a lady, so treat me like one*. What do you think?"

"Yeah, that's nice." She smiled softly.

"Good, now come here." Kathy pulled Randi to her and hugged her tightly. "You can do this, Randi. I know you can."

Chapter 9

A week later, after her shift was over, Randi rushed home to get dressed for her date. She washed her hair in the shower and allowed it to air dry. It poured down her shoulders into tiny curls. She slipped on the cream-colored pantsuit that she had purchased. It fell gently over her curves. As she applied her makeup, she thought about the conversation she had had with her friend. Kathy was right. She could do this. After all, it was only a date. He hadn't proposed. And although she hadn't convinced herself that she would continue seeing him after their date, she couldn't deny that she was feeling him.

Take it slow, Randi, she told herself. *Take it really slow. Don't get caught up in his fame and his money. You're going out with Anthony Talbert, not Animalistic.* Just as she put on the last touches of her makeup, there was a knock at the door. She looked at her watch. It was 10:00 exactly. He was punctual, and she liked that.

As she headed for the door, her heart started to race. She was both nervous and excited about seeing him again. *Calm down,* she told herself. She stood at the door a second before she opened it. *It's only a date,* she told herself. *It's only a little date.* "Then why are you so damn scared?" she whispered. She took a deep breath then opened the door.

Anthony stood there so tall and commanding. He was beautiful. He wore a tan, super-soft silk and cashmere Armani suit. He didn't look like a rapper; he looked more like a male model. His eyes lit up when he saw her. He smiled approvingly. They stared at each other in silence for a second or two.

"You look beautiful," he said as he started to get nervous.

"Thank you." She blushed. "You look very nice too."

"Oh, um, these are for you." He handed her a bouquet of white roses.

"Thank you. They're beautiful." She took them and stepped back for him to enter. "Let me put these in some water and I'll be ready to go."

He watched her as she went into the kitchen. Her suit fit her perfectly, accentuating her waist and hips. *Damn,* he said to himself. He could see his confirmed bachelorhood going down the drain with this girl, and he didn't mind.

Neither one of them said a word as they headed for the car. Once they slipped inside, Randi finally spoke. "Is something wrong? You're quiet."

He looked over at her. "You make me nervous," he admitted.

"Nervous. Why?" She was surprised.

"Not counting breakfast, it's been six years since I've been on a date," he explained as they pulled off into the night.

"Six years," Randi repeated.

"And the fact that you're so damn perfect scares me. I don't want to fu—I mean screw this up."

"Thanks, but I'm hardly perfect."

"What's wrong with you then? From where I'm sitting, you look perfect to me." He looked over at her.

She blushed again. Twice in one night, that was a record. "I don't cook."

"We'll work on that." He smiled and turned his eyes back to the road. "I've made reservations for us, so I hope you're hungry."

"I did eat a little something at work."

"You didn't think I would take you out and not feed you, did you?" He chuckled and began to loosen up.

"It wouldn't be the first time." She smiled.

"Really? Then you've been going out with the wrong guys. You're with the right one now."

Randi became puzzled when he turned into the parking lot of a small, independent airport.

"Hold on." He got out of the car and ran over to a man who stood in the parking lot smoking a cigarette.

Randi watched as they exchanged a few words. The man threw his cigarette down and stepped on it before he climbed into a small Beech Jet 400. Anthony ran back over to the car and opened her door.

She got out. "What's going on?" she asked.

After he closed the door behind her, he slipped his hand into hers and led her over to the jet.

"You aren't afraid of flying, are you?" he asked. "I know it's small, but it's safe."

"No, but what are you doing?"

"We've got dinner reservations in one hour in Atlanta."

"Atlanta? Are you serious?"

"Yep." He started up the stairs of the jet and pulled her along.

She pulled back. "But I—"

He stopped and turned around to face her. "What's wrong?"

"Are, are we really doing this? Are we really flying to Atlanta for dinner?"

"Yes, ma'am."

"But this is so unreal. It's like something out of a movie."

"Well, it's real, baby. It's just one of the perks of dating a rap star, so get used to being treated like a princess."

"I can't believe this is happening." She smiled.

"Are you impressed?"

"Yes."

"Good. So, are we doing this?"

"Yeah." She nodded as her smile grew bigger. "Yes, yes, we're doing this."

"Ladies first." He stepped back and held his hand out so she could go up.

They climbed into the small aircraft. Although Randi had flown before, she had never been inside a private jet. She looked around. It was small and cozy. The interior was a pale, relaxing color from the walls to the carpet to the soft leather captain's chairs that surrounded a small table. The plane included a small refrigerator and a flat-screen TV to keep passengers fed and entertained during their flight.

Randi smiled as she took in all of this. This was some fancy lifestyle, she thought as she took a seat in one of the captain's chairs. The comfortable seat was so large that it almost swallowed her tiny frame. Anthony sat down across from her.

"You want something to drink?" he asked.

"No, thank you." She looked around the plane then back at him. "This is really, really nice."

"This is what I flew down here to see you in," he said.

"Really? I guess you fly a lot."

"Not really. We travel on our bus when we're doing concerts, but for special occasions like this, I rent a jet."

"This is a special occasion?" she asked.

"This is our first official date."

"Oh. You've gone through a lot of trouble for this date."

Debra Clayton

"It's worth the trouble, and I hope there's many more."

She smiled nervously as she watched him. He was so charming and so handsome and so rich. She had to keep reminding herself why she couldn't just drop her defenses and go for it. "Maybe."

The jet ride was smooth and quick. After they landed, they got into another car and drove to the restaurant, which appeared to be closed. There were only two cars in the parking lot, and the building appeared almost completely dark.

"We must be too late. They look closed," she said.

"Let's hope not." He got out of the car, walked over to her side, and opened her door.

When they reached the restaurant, the front door was unlocked. They stepped inside. The restaurant was quiet and empty. In one of the corners was a small round table with a candle flickering in the center. It was set for two. Anthony put his hand on the small of her back and guided her through the room to the table. He pulled the chair out for her and she sat down then took his seat across from her.

"You planned this?" she whispered.

He nodded with a smile.

A second later, a waiter came out and filled their water glasses. He gave them menus and took their drink orders. Randi watched Anthony while he looked over his menu. She didn't know what to think. This guy was definitely trying to sweep her off her feet, and he wasn't doing a bad job of it.

He looked up and caught her watching him. "What's wrong?" he asked.

"I just can't get over tonight. I can't believe you did all this." The candlelight danced across her face. She was smiling.

"I can't believe you did all this," he whispered.

"What?" She didn't understand.

82

The waiter reappeared with their drinks and took their orders.

"What did I do?" she asked after the waiter left.

Their eyes met. "You knocked me off my feet. I'm just trying to return the favor."

Girl, if you blush one more time I'm going to pinch you, she told herself as she felt herself turning red again.

"This place is beautiful," she said as she looked around.

"You like it?"

"Yeah, I do." She paused. "It must be really nice to be able to afford to do all this."

"It is. Money is great. Success is wonderful. But you know, at the end of the day, it doesn't matter how much money or fame you have. At the end of the day, when the fans have gone home and the coliseums are closed, when the groupies have gotten what they wanted and you go home, you're alone."

"So, you get lonely?" She never thought about that side of fame.

"Yeah, I get lonely sometimes."

"I just assumed that with people constantly clamoring after you, you wouldn't get lonely."

"What about you? You ever get lonely?" he asked.

"Yeah, a lot."

"Two lonely hearts in search of love, meet finally face to face."

"The happiness and joy I'd lost, I've found in your embrace." She finished the line for him.

Impressed, he smiled. " 'The Longest Night' by Mr. Montell Jordan. You're good."

"Well, I've been a fan of Montell's for about as long as I've been a fan of yours."

"Well, it's a good thing I met you before he did."

"Actually, I know more about you than Montell."

"Well, impress me then."

"Okay. Let's see. You were born Anthony Lamar Talbert to a Paul and Sylvia Talbert in Des Moines, Iowa. You are the youngest of two kids. You have an older brother named Michael. Although you would rather be singing, you broke into the rap industry in 1998 when you were only eighteen. Your first CD was *Now Hear This,* which went platinum. In 2000, you released *All I Need* and then in 2002 you released *This Way Us,* both of which went multi-platinum. In 2004, you released *A Lover and a Fighter,* which has also reached multi-platinum status. Of all your songs, 'You Know How We Do' is your favorite, and your least favorite is 'Roll With Me.' So, how am I doing?"

"That was an impressive body of knowledge. And I mean impressive body."

"Why, thank you." She smiled and nodded.

"You know, I'm looking at you and I'm wondering why you listen to my music. The way you look, the way you talk, the way you carry yourself, it's hard to believe that you listen to hip-hop."

"I know. I get that a lot. The thing that draws me to hip-hop is the lyrics. Since I'm a writer, words are very important to me, and some of the hip-hop songs have the most incredible lyrics. I mean, some rappers have got crazy skills when it comes to their lyrics. Rappers like Tupac, Fabolous, Lloyd Banks, Eminem, and of course yourself. Your lyrics are nasty."

"Nasty. I like that." He took a sip of his wine. "So, are you enjoying yourself so far?"

"I am."

"So, this isn't the worst date you've ever been on?"

"Hardly. My worst date . . . " She shook her head.

"Tell me about it."

She watched his smile as she thought it over. "When I was about seventeen, this guy took me to his house and we watched television in his living room."

"And?"

"His parents were in the other room watching porn and getting high. They asked us if we wanted to join them. He said yeah and I said no, then I ran for the nearest exit."

By the time she finished, he was laughing out loud. "Are you serious?"

"As a heart attack."

He took a sip of his wine, sat back and watched her. She needed to laugh more often.

"So, what about you? What was your worst date?" he asked.

He thought for a moment. The waiter returned with their food.

"I never really had a bad date, but I did have a bad morning after."

"Tell me." She leaned forward.

"I was about sixteen and I took this girl out. We slept together on our first date. The next morning when I woke up, I was burning," he confessed.

"Eeww." She made a face. She was surprised by his honesty.

"From that point on, I've always used protection." He cut into his steak.

"At least you learned something from it," she teased as she took a bite of her salmon. "So, have you ever had your heart broken?"

"Never," he said after swallowing.

"I guess that would mean that you've never been in

85

love before." She watched for his response.

He looked up from his food. "Never." He waited to see what she was going to say.

"Man. So, nobody's ever gotten to you, huh?"

He looked her in her eyes. "You get to me."

She stared back. *You get to me,* she thought. She finally tore her eyes away and focused on her food.

"I didn't mean to make you uncomfortable." He sensed her uneasiness.

"You didn't." She looked up at him and smiled. "I'm just not ready for any of this."

"Why not?" What was she running from?

"I've just got a lot of personal issues that I need to work out."

"Like what?"

"They're personal."

"Talk to me, Randi."

"I can't," she insisted.

"What in the hell did he do to you?"

"I'm not ready to talk to you about it yet. I'm just not ready."

"Okay, okay, I won't pressure you. It's just that I'm starting to catch feelings for you, and you just keep pushing me away."

"Just give me some time."

"I can try, but I have to know that I'm getting somewhere with you. I have to know that you're feeling something."

"I am," she admitted.

"Now, that's what I'm talking about."

After they finished dinner, soft music began to play. *Right on cue,* Anthony thought. To their left, a spotlight came on and lit up the stage. Singer Kevin Rivers stepped into the light and began to serenade them with love songs. His first song was Ruff Endz's "Someone to Love You." Randi's mouth dropped open as she looked at Kevin then Anthony, who smiled as he watched the expression on her face.

"I can't believe you did this," she whispered as she stared at him. No one had ever done anything like this for her. She was overwhelmed as she fought to keep herself from crying.

Without a word, Anthony stood up, moved to her side, and held out his hand for her. She took it and stood up. He gently pulled her to him. Her arms automatically went up and around his neck as she pressed her head against his chest. His arms encircled her waist; his hands rested on the small of her back. They swayed to the slow rhythm of the music. His body felt hard and strong as she lay against him. His scent filled her nostrils. He smelled delicious, she thought. She felt surprisingly comfortable in his arms.

So, this is what it feels like to hold her, he thought. She felt so tiny and fragile. He held her gently as if not to break her. She was so different from the women he was used to and he liked her frailty. He wanted to protect her. He wanted to wipe away all her bad memories and replace them with nights like this one. He wanted to keep her and never give her back. His lips came down next to her ear.

"Can I keep you forever?" he whispered. His breath was warm on her skin.

She looked up at him and wondered how she had gotten there. She wondered how, after so many nights of crying and so many nights of screaming and so many nights of loneliness, she had ended up in this wonderful man's arms. Was he real or was he just another one of her characters that had somehow come to life, if only for one night? Maybe she had written this scene herself. Maybe she had placed herself in

87

his arms. She didn't know how she had gotten there, but she knew that she did want to stay there forever. "Yes," she responded. "Yes, you can keep me forever."

Anthony brought his hand up to her face as he thought about his no kissing rule. There were no rules when it came to Randi, he told himself. He slowly dragged his thumb over her lips as he wondered if they tasted as sweet as they looked. Slowly, he lowered his head, pulled her face closer, and allowed his lips to gently brush over hers. Patiently, cautiously, he kissed her as he waited for her response.

Randi slightly parted her lips as she kissed him back. She marveled at the tenderness in his touch as his tongue entered her mouth to taste her. Wanting more, he pulled her closer and their kiss deepened. He felt himself slipping away as he savored the sweet warmth of her mouth. *Remarkable,* he thought as his hand slid down to the small of her back and pressed her hips to his. He felt himself becoming aroused and he fought the urge to let his hands explore more. Fearing that he would offend her, he slowly, reluctantly pulled away from her.

Randi stared up at him in awe. He had kissed her. She had been kissed by Animalistic. She couldn't believe it. She couldn't believe the sweet, warm tenderness that his lips held. She couldn't believe how gentle and non-invading his hands were on her body. Over a month ago, he was asking her for a blow-job; tonight he gently held her in his arms and kissed her like he was her prince charming. She could really fall for him.

"That wasn't too much for you to handle, was it?" He hoped he hadn't gone too far.

"No." She shook her head.

"Good." He pulled her back into his arms and they began to dance again. " 'Cause I could really get used to kissing you."

"Me too," she whispered as she allowed herself to melt into his arms.

After they danced for what seemed like hours, he said in a barely audible voice, "I guess I should be getting you home." He didn't want the evening to end, but he knew that he couldn't keep her out all night.

Reluctantly, she pulled away from his arms.

"I guess you should," she agreed. She looked up at him. How could this man be the same guy she met at that party? He had changed so much. She turned away, picked up her purse and they left.

They reached the jet and boarded it.

"Tell me about your family," he said once they were in the air. "Are your mom and dad still around?"

"Yeah, but they aren't together. Dad lives in Virginia. That's where I'm from originally. Mom lives in North Carolina. She moved us there when she left my father," Randi answered.

"Was it hard when they split up?"

"Yeah, it was, but I got over it. When you're young, you're very resilient."

"Good. They get along?"

"Yeah. I think they get along better now that they're divorced."

He laughed, watching her as she pushed her hair away from her face and smiled at him "Damn, you're beautiful, girl," he said.

She blushed again and pinched herself.

"What was that for?" he asked.

"For blushing," she admitted.

"Do I make you blush?"

"Yes."

"Does that mean you like me, just a little?"

"Just a little." She smiled.

After they got off the jet, he drove her home.

"Sorry I got you home so late." He apologized as they stood in front of her apartment door.

"Don't apologize. I had a great time." She looked up at him with her key in her hand.

"May I?" he asked, taking the keys. She watched as he unlocked the door. She was sure he would invite himself in, but he didn't. He turned back around and handed her the key.

"I guess we'll be going out again?" He looked down at her.

"I guess so," she said with a smile.

"I'll check my schedule and call you this week. Maybe we'll be able to set something up." He brought his hand up to her cheek, caressing it. He looked into her eyes as if trying to see her soul. "I guess I have to say good night," he whispered.

"Would you like to come in for a little while?"

"Actually I would, but the way I'm feeling right now, holding your hand and talking wouldn't be enough for me," he said as he fought the urge to satisfy his own desires. He didn't want to rush her. *Walk away, man,* he told himself. *She's not ready for this*.

"Okay, I understand."

"I'll call you," he said as he pulled his hand away from her face.

"Okay," she managed to mutter.

He turned and walked away. She watched him as he disappeared then she entered her apartment.

Once in her bedroom, she slipped out of her clothes and climbed into bed. *Tonight was perfect,* she thought. He had made her feel beautiful. She thought about their dancing, about how good it felt to be in his arms, pressed up against his body. His cologne still lingered on her skin. She was surprised by his behavior. He was a perfect gentleman the whole night.

She lay in the darkness and thought about him. Then in revelation, she sat up in the bed. What was she doing? She wasn't supposed to let things go this far. He was so smooth that he had slipped in under her radar. She realized that she was letting herself fall for this guy. She couldn't do that. She couldn't fall for him. It was too dangerous. She had to regain control over the situation. She couldn't get caught up. She knew what she had to do.

The next day, Randi told Kathy everything that happened on their date.

"So, when is the next one?" Kathy asked.

"He said he would call me, but I can't go out with him again."

"Not because of Eric?"

"It's everything. It's the groupies and the intimacy and the trust issues. If I fell in love with him, Kathy, and he cheated on me with one of those groupies, I'd die."

"He's obviously feeling something for you. Why would he cheat on you?"

"Eric felt something for me but he cheated on me. And what about the sex? How am I supposed to be able to satisfy someone who I may not be able to have sex with? And if I can sleep with him, then how am I supposed to be able to satisfy someone who's used to being with a lot of experienced women? My only sexual experience was with Eric. I would never be able to keep Anthony satisfied. And why should he go without when he has all these beautiful women ready and willing to do anything that he asks of them?"

"You can't live life like this, Randi. You're not even giving him a chance. Because of Eric, you've already written this guy off. He's really trying, and you keep pushing him away. Randi, you've been alone for over a year now. You haven't let anybody get this close to you since Eric. You need to stop this."

Randi continued to listen to Kathy as she scolded her.

"Girl, I love you. I think you're beautiful and you're one of the kindest people I know, but you have to get over this. Give this guy a chance."

"I can't. I just can't."

"Eric really did a number on you, didn't he?"

"You were there. You saw what he did to me." She cringed as the memories of that evening came flooding back.

She could still feel the painful blows against her body as he pummeled her. She could still taste her own blood which covered her face, and still see him unfastening his pants just before he forced himself on her. She could still feel his hands around her neck when she tried to scream for help, and then everything went black.

She remembered waking up in the hospital with a broken and bruised body. She suffered from cracked ribs, a broken jaw, blackened eyes, and a concussion. The police charged him with simple assault. He only got a year and a half for nearly killing her.

"Yes, I was there," Kathy said. "I found you, and I'm the one who dialed 911. I saw what he did to you. I thought you were dead.

"Your body healed, but your heart didn't. I see what he's doing to you now, Randi. He's killing you every day by killing all possibilities of you ever being happy again. Let him go, Randi. Just let him go."

Randi swallowed as she tried to keep herself from

crying. She knew Kathy was right, but she wasn't ready to get back out there, to put her heart back on the line.

"I've gotta go, Kathy," she lied. She didn't want to talk to her friend anymore.

"Randi, don't hang up."

"I've gotta go." She hung up, pulled her knees to her chest and wrapped her arms around them, as if in an attempt to protect herself. She took a deep breath, closed her eyes and bit her bottom lip. She continued trying to hold back the tears but she couldn't stop them. They swelled up behind her eyelids, seeped out and trickled down her face. She knew she couldn't see Anthony anymore. She just hoped that it wasn't too late.

Chapter 10

The crowd roared as Anthony dashed off stage after his last performance. He had agreed to do the last-minute performance for the Atlanta "A Home for the Homeless" benefit concert only after he couldn't set up another date with Randi. It had been three weeks since their date in Atlanta, and even though he called nearly every day, he couldn't get a straight answer from her about why she couldn't go out with him again. She always said that she was busy, but he knew it was a lie. He was the one with the busy schedule as he raced off to shoot videos, perform at events, and record his latest CD. If he could find time to see her, then surely she could take a break from her job to make time to see him.

He pushed his way through the crowd backstage as he tried to make sense of her actions. One minute she was in his arms kissing him, and the next she was running away from him. His patience was wearing thin with her inconsistencies. He wanted to talk to her and find out what was really going on with her. As he slipped past the other performers, he ignored their attempts to get his attention. His mind was on Randi.

Once he reached his dressing room, he darted inside and went straight for the phone.

"Hello," Randi said as she answered the phone.

"What in the hell's going on, Randi? Did I do something wrong?" he asked.

It's him again, she thought. She could tell he was not in a good mood, and she knew it was because of her. "No."

"Listen, I've been calling for three weeks now to get another date with you, and you keep brushing me off. What's up with that? I thought we had a good time."

"We did. I had a wonderful time, but—"

"Then why are you avoiding me? You told me I could keep you forever."

"I know, but I was just caught up in the moment. I didn't mean it."

"So, you don't care about me?"

"Why are you doing this, Anthony? I told you I have issues to work through. I don't need all of this pressure on me."

"Well, I'll tell you what I don't need, Randi," he said, becoming even more heated. "I don't need you to keep jerking me around like this. I'm running all over trying to get to you. I've given up all these hoes to be with you, and all you can do is push me away and say you don't need the pressure. I don't have to put up with this shit. Do you hear me?"

"I never asked you to put up with me, Anthony. I never asked you to call. I never asked you to come by. I never asked you for anything. You're the one who insisted on being a part of my life."

"Well, I'll tell you what. You don't want me in your life, then I'm gone. Is that what you want? Huh? Is that what you want? You want me to leave you the hell alone?"

"Yes," Randi said as tears streamed down her face.

Anthony slammed down the receiver. "Fuck!" he yelled. He paced the floor as he tried to figure out what to do next. Why in the hell was she acting like this? He had to get out to get some fresh air. He headed for the door. If she didn't want to be with him, he knew somebody who did. He knew plenty of women who would love to be in her place. He knew plenty of women who would love to be in his bed. He didn't need this shit from some country-ass chick in North Carolina.

A determined Anthony stepped out into the night air. The streets were still crowded as performers waited for their limos and security held back star-struck fans who struggled to get a good glimpse of their favorite performers.

"We love you, Animalistic!" a group of young women yelled as they frantically tried to get his attention.

He gave them a quick wave of acknowledgement as he waited for his driver. The girls went crazy when they saw that he had noticed them. His driver pulled up and he slipped in the back seat of his limo. As he sunk down into the seat and enjoyed the benefits of his wealth and fame, his mind quickly went to Randi and their conversation. He didn't have time for her silly excuses. He was tired of trying to chase her down. If she wanted him out of her life, then he was ghost. She wouldn't have to worry about him anymore.

As the driver pulled the limo out into traffic, Anthony told him to stop near a group of young ladies standing near the curb. The driver pulled over, lowered his window, and gestured for the girls to come over.

"Mr. Animalistic has requested your company," the driver informed the one that Anthony had picked out. "Are you interested?"

"Oh yes," the girl squealed with excitement as her friends clamored around her with the same enthusiasm.

The driver slipped out of the car and walked the young lady to the back door of the limo. Anthony sat back and took in all the excitement. He wondered why Randi never got that excited about him. He knew that she had to have something that she was hiding inside her that wouldn't let her just enjoy him. He knew that she must have been hurting inside, but if she didn't open up and share, then he could do nothing to help her. He had to move on.

The driver opened the door and the young lady peered inside. Her eyes grew large with excitement and she looked at Anthony. She could barely believe her luck. Anthony gestured for her to come in. She quickly slipped into the leather seat of the limo. "Oh my God," she mouthed, but nothing came out. She was in awe as her eyes absorbed the luxuries of the limousine.

"What's your name?" Anthony asked as his eyes traveled over her curvaceous figure, which her tiny black dress barely covered. She would do for tonight, he thought. She was just what he needed to get his mind off of Randi.

"Asia Tyler." She smiled. "I'm a huge fan of yours. I just love your music."

"Thanks," he said as he brought his eyes up from her plump, round breasts to her angelic face. Although she looked like an angel, he was sure that she was not one. "So, Asia Tyler, you want to get fucked by a superstar?"

Asia smiled confidently. She knew his intentions before she stepped into the limousine. He wouldn't be the first rapper she fucked, and she didn't plan on him being the last. "Why the hell not?" She crossed her legs, showing him just enough skin to whet his appetite.

"Now, that's what I like," he said with a smile. "A woman who knows what she wants."

A few minutes later, Anthony and Asia had checked into a nearby hotel. He didn't have time to take her back to his hotel. He wanted to fuck her as soon as possible.

"Just let me freshen up," Asia said

"Go ahead. I'll fix us some drinks," he said as he walked over to the mini bar. "What are you drinking?"

"I'll take a Fuzzy Navel," Asia said as she slipped into the bathroom.

"Cool," he said as he fixed their drinks. He started to think about Randi, but quickly tried to push her out of his head. He didn't want her anywhere around tonight. If she didn't want him around, then he didn't want her. He was gonna have a good time tonight. He was gonna fuck Asia like he should have been fucking all those groupies that he had given up for Randi. Did she not know what he had given up for her? Did she not know how much he had sacrificed and how much he cared for her? Women were throwing pussy at him left, right and center, and all he got from Randi were excuses why she couldn't see him again. He definitely didn't need that shit. What he needed was a blow-job and a good fuck.

***

Kathy entered Randi's apartment. Randi was sitting on the sofa with her knees pulled up to her chest, hugging her legs. Her tear-covered face was swollen. Kathy walked over to her and sat down. She pushed Randi's hair back out of her face. Randi blinked, and more tears raced down her face.

"You didn't have to push him away, baby," Kathy said. She felt sorry for her friend. It was obvious that she was falling in love with Anthony, even if she wouldn't admit it.

"This is for the best," Randi whispered.

"How can you say that? Look at how you're hurting now. How is this for the best?"

"Six months from now, it would hurt worse. Six months from now when he decides that I'm not enough for him; six months from now when I'm madly in love with him; six months from now when he wants to walk away from me, it will hurt a whole lot worse than it does now."

"Baby, you can't look at it that way. You've got to believe in the relationship. You've got to believe in you and him. You gotta love, baby, like you're never gonna get hurt."

"Well, it doesn't matter now. He's gone. He's gone out

of my life." Her lip trembled as she started to cry harder.

Kathy slid over next to her and pulled her into her arms. "I'm not leaving you alone tonight."

***

"I hope you're ready for me," Asia said as she stepped out of the bathroom wearing nothing but a smile.

Anthony turned around and looked the leggy beauty as she walked toward him. Without a word, he handed her a drink. He didn't want to talk. All he wanted to do was fuck her like she had never been fucked before.

"Why aren't you undressed?" she asked as she took her drink.

"I'm just moving a little slow tonight, that's all."

"Well, I hope you're not moving too slow." She took a sip of her drink then set down the glass. "Now, let me make you a little less restricted." She started unbuttoning his shirt. As she revealed the smooth skin of his chest, she covered it with soft, wet kisses.

Still nursing his drink, he closed his eyes as Asia squatted in front of him and started working on his belt. He thought about Randi. She should have been the one undoing his clothes. She should have been the one that was getting ready to make love to him. It should have been her hands on his bare skin, not Asia's. The sound of his jeans being unzipped made him open his eyes. He grabbed Asia's hand as he looked down at her.

Surprised, she looked up at him. "Is everything okay?"

Suddenly, he felt like he was doing something wrong. He didn't want to do this. Randi was hurting, and instead of finding out what it was that she was going through, he was up in a hotel room with some chick whose name he couldn't even remember.

He didn't really want to fuck this girl. He wanted to find Randi and make her tell him what the hell was going on with her. He wanted to find out why she was really running away from him and make her stop. He had to talk to her. Before he truly walked out of her life, he had to see her. He had to talk to her face to face and make sure this was what she wanted. He wasn't ready to give up on her yet. He wasn't ready to give up on them.

He put his glass down and pulled Asia up. "I'm sorry, sweetie, but I have to leave."

"Right now?" She looked puzzled.

"Yeah, right now. It can't wait."

"Just like that? You got me standing here butt-naked in front of you and you're telling me that you have to leave."

"I gotta go take care of some business. The room's paid for, so enjoy."

"I don't believe this bullshit," she said, placing her hand on her hip. "I coulda been fucking Kobe Bryant by now."

"Thanks for understanding." He pulled up his zipper and left. He had to hurry back to his hotel and pack. He was going to Greensboro, North Carolina.

Chapter 11

A couple of hours later, a loud banging on the door awakened the girls. Randi rolled over and looked at the clock. It was 2:38 a.m.

"Who in the hell could that be?" Kathy asked as she sat up in the bed and looked over at Randi.

"I don't know." She climbed out of bed, slipped on her robe, and hurried down the hall. Kathy followed.

"Who is it?" Randi asked midway through a yawn.

"It's me. Anthony."

"Anthony," she whispered as she looked at Kathy. "What is he doing here?" She didn't want to see him. He said he was gone out of her life, and now he was back. Why was he back? Why was he trying to make this so hard for her?

"Open the door, Randi," Kathy said.

"I can't. I don't want to see him."

"You need to talk to him. He wants to talk to you."

"Why doesn't he just leave me alone?"

"Because he cares about you." She grabbed Randi's arm. "Listen, if you don't open the door, I will. I promise you, Randi. I will," she threatened. She hated putting her friend in that spot, but she felt that Randi wasn't thinking clearly. She was too emotional to know what was best for her. If she wasn't going to willingly talk to Anthony, then Kathy would make her.

"Randi, you might as well open the door. I'm not leaving here until I talk to you. I've come too far to leave without seeing you," Anthony demanded. He was tired of accommodating her. She was gonna have to put up with him until he was satisfied with her explanation for running away from him.

"At least hear him out, Randi," Kathy urged.

Randi stared at Kathy. "I can't."

"You can."

She stared down at the doorknob.

"I've got all day, baby," he informed her as he prepared himself to take a seat outside of her door. "You can either open the door, talk to me and get it over with, or I can sit out here all day long waiting for you. It's up to you."

She looked at Kathy. "What am I supposed to say to him?"

"Tell him how you feel. Tell him what's going on inside you. He deserves that. Don't just shut him out."

Kathy was right. Anthony had been so patient with her. He had taken time out of his hectic schedule to see her and to show her an incredible time. He was putting so much effort into being with her. The least she could do was talk to him.

"Talk to him," Kathy said.

"Okay." She nodded. "I'll talk to him."

She opened the door. The look on his face revealed that he was more than frustrated with the situation. She understood. She was frustrated with herself as well. She knew she could have handled the situation better than she had. She should have just stayed away from him. She should have just refused to go out with him, but her heart and her head were in constant battle over what she should do about him.

Without saying a word, Anthony walked past Kathy and Randi and took a seat on the couch. He picked a magazine off the coffee table and started flipping through it.

"I was just leaving," Kathy said as she touched

Randi's arm. "You talk to him and explain everything to him."

Randi nodded.

While Kathy disappeared into the bedroom to get dressed, Randi walked over and sat down across from Anthony. She watched him as he continued to feign interest in the magazine articles. They both sat in silence as they waited for Kathy to leave.

Minutes later, Kathy reentered the living room fully dressed. "Hey, guys, I'm gonna let myself out. Randi, I'll talk to you later. Anthony, it was good seeing you."

"Wait a minute," Anthony said as he tossed the magazine back down on the coffee table and stood up. "Let me walk you out."

He walked Kathy to her car while Randi waited for him.

"Anthony," Kathy said before getting into her car. "She really cares about you, even if she won't admit it. She's just scared. But no matter what she does, don't leave here until she tells you what's going on."

He nodded. "Thanks, Kathy."

After Kathy drove off, he ran back upstairs to Randi.

"Okay, now tell me what the hell is going on," he demanded as he sat back down. He was tired of handling her with kid gloves. His patience was worn, and he was sick of playing games. He stared at her as he searched her small face for an answer. "I know you care about me. Why the hell do you keep running from me?"

She could hear the frustration in his voice. She couldn't blame him for what he was feeling. "It's like I told you, Anthony. I have a lot of issues I need to work through."

"No," he said as he stood up and looked down at her. "That's weak. That's too weak an answer. I didn't fly all the way over here to hear that same weak-ass excuse. I deserve more than that. What in the hell is going on?" he demanded.

She looked up at him and shook her head. "It's so much, Anthony. It's so much." She bit her bottom lip as she tried not to cry.

He knew she was hurting. He knelt down in front of her and took her hand. "Baby, what the hell did he do to you?" He searched her eyes for an answer.

She quickly turned her face away from his, but he placed one hand on her chin and gently guided her face back to his. "Talk to me, baby," he said. His voice was much softer.

Randi's lip quivered as tears swelled up in her eyes. "He took everything away from me," she finally managed.

"How? What did he do?"

"We were high school sweethearts," she said as she wiped away the tears that were perched to race down her cheeks. "I know it sounds like a cliché, but we were."

"Okay." He nodded.

"He was really possessive. I gave up my family and friends and my dreams for him."

Anthony gently squeezed her hand to reassure her that it was okay to go on.

"We got engaged and moved in together." She swallowed. "One day, while he was at work, I got a call from a girl saying she was six months pregnant by him."

"Damn," Anthony said as he watched the pain on her face.

"He didn't even deny it." She blinked, and more tears spilled down her cheeks.

He reached up and gently wiped the tears away with his thumb. "I am so sorry," he whispered. "He was an idiot, baby." He was beginning to understand her pain.

Randi closed her eyes tightly as she remembered that night. She didn't want to fall apart in front of him. As she tried to regain strength, she opened her eyes and looked at him. She was unsure whether she should tell him the whole story, but she wanted to. She wanted him to understand why she couldn't be with him. "I tried to leave him that night," she continued. "But he wouldn't let me."

Anthony quietly listened.

She brought her hands up to cover her face. She knew she was about to break down, and she didn't want Anthony to see her. "He tried to kill me," she whispered as her hands began trembling and tears raced down her face.

"Damn," was all he could say as he pulled her into his arms. She buried her face in his chest as she wept. He squeezed her trembling body against him.

"He beat me and raped me and tried to kill me." She sobbed as she clung to him.

Anthony closed his eyes and kissed the top of her head as he felt a rage building in him. He clutched her to him as he tried not to lose it. How could a man hit a woman? How could he rape a woman? Women were the weaker sex. Only a coward would do this. Only a punk-ass coward would put his hands on a woman. The longer he held her trembling body, the angrier he grew. He wanted to find this guy. He wanted to find the guy who had caused her so much pain, the guy who had damaged her heart and her soul and her spirit.

As Randi's crying began to diminish, he loosened his grip on her. He stroked her hair. Now he understood why she was hurting so much. "I'm glad you told me," he whispered.

She slowly pulled away from him and looked up at him. "Do you understand now why I can't be with you?

"I understand why you're hurting so much, but it doesn't change the way I feel about you. I still want to be with you Ran—"

"You don't understand," she cut him off.

He stared down at her tear-stained face. He was confused. "Then make me. Explain it to me."

"After what I've been through, how could I trust you? How would I be able to trust you, Anthony? I've only been with one man, and he cheated on me and then raped me. You're constantly on the road, surrounded by beautiful women who are willing to do anything for you. I don't know if I could satisfy you. I wouldn't even know how to satisfy you. I don't even know if I could be intimate with you. You've had all kinds of women, Anthony. Why would I expect you to be satisfied with me?"

It all finally made sense to him.

"I could fall for you. I could really fall hard for you and what—" He paused, tilted her face up to his and shook his head. "Damn, it, Randi. I've already fell. Don't you know that?"

"But what about my issues?"

"They're our issues, and we'll work through them one day at a time. I don't want you and me anymore. I want *us*. I want to be with you. Just give us a try, Randi. We'll take it slowly. I won't put any pressure on you. You set the pace and I'll go with it. I'm just not ready to let you walk away from this. Just give us a try."

"And you're willing to put up with my insecurities?"

"Yes. Baby, I have never met anyone like you. You are the only woman that wasn't mesmerized by my stardom. You are the only one that wouldn't lower your morals just to appease me. You treated me like a regular guy, and I appreciate that. I know why you want to be with me. It's not because I'm Animalistic. You want to be with Anthony Talbert. All these other chicks want to be with the rapper. You want to be with the man. I trust you. And I've never been able to trust any of these other women. You also push me to be better than I was. You made me reevaluate the way I was living, and all in all, you make me wanna be a better man. Baby, you make me a better man."

"I did all that?"

"Yes. I put away my whorish ways because I want to be with you. No one else could make me do that."

He was telling the truth and she knew it. She had seen the changes in him. It was the changes that made her want to be with him. He had grown so much since their first encounter.

"So, what do you say, Randi? Give us a try?"

"And we'll take it slow?"

"As slow as you want it, baby. I won't rush you. Any time you feel uncomfortable with the rate things are moving, just let me know and we can slow it down even more. Okay?"

"Okay." She nodded and smiled.

Anthony kissed her they embraced.

After Anthony finally released her, she looked up at him. "Do you have to leave?" she asked. It had been so long since she had seen him. She missed him and wanted him to stay longer.

"Not 'til about six in the morning. Do you mind if I stay? I haven't had any sleep."

"No." She wanted him to stay.

"Do you mind if I lay down with you?"

"I um…" She became uneasy at his request.

"I just want to hold you, that's all. Nothing else."

Seeing the sincerity in his eyes and hearing it in his voice, she knew she could trust him. "That's fine." She smiled.

Anthony followed Randi as she led him to her bedroom. After taking off her robe, she climbed into bed and slid under the covers. Anthony slipped off his shoes and climbed onto the bed next to her, however, he lay on top of the covers. He didn't want to make her too uncomfortable. *Take it slowly,* he told himself. He lay on his back and gently pulled her over to him until she was in his arms. She rested her head on his chest and draped her arm around his waist.

Her body molded against his perfectly, Anthony thought as he held her. He had never held a woman like this before. This was so different from what he was used to. Normally he would just fuck, nut, roll over and fall asleep. This was what he had been looking for all this time and he hadn't even known it.

"Randi," he whispered.

"Yes."

"So, where is your ex now?" He wanted to make sure this guy was long gone. He wanted to make sure he wouldn't hurt her ever again.

"He's serving an eighteen-month sentence."

"Eighteen months," he said in disbelief. "Is that all he got?"

"Yeah. They charged him with assault, but not for the rape. He denied raping me, and they said since we lived together at the time, the rape was too hard to prove."

"You'll never ever have to worry about me hurting you like that. I would never put my hands on you like that."

"I know," she whispered as she closed her eyes. She marveled at how surprisingly comfortable she felt lying there in his arms. It had been a lifetime since someone held her like that. She could do this forever, she thought.

The next morning when Anthony awoke, he realized that they changed positions. Randi had rolled over and curled up. He had curled up behind her with his arm draped around her waist. She was still asleep. The warm feelings of the night before seeped back into his memory. He smiled and gently squeezed her. He glanced at the clock. It was 8:00. His flight had left two hours ago. He knew Thomas was going to be pissed, but he didn't give a damn. Thomas would just have to get over it.

He carefully pulled his arm from around her waist, trying not to disturb her. He rolled over onto his back, then on to his other side and slipped out of the bed. She stirred slightly but didn't wake up. He paused for a few seconds, watched her sleep, then disappeared into the bathroom.

After he relieved himself, he washed his face. Minutes later, he walked over to her side of the bed and stooped down in front of her. She snored lightly. He chuckled. She didn't look like the snoring type. He gently pushed her hair back, exposing more of her face then leaned over gently kissed her forehead.

"Thank you," he whispered. He left the room only to return with a note to place on the pillow.

When Randi woke up, he was already gone. She felt a twinge of sadness. He was probably in the air by now. She smiled when she spotted the note he left for her.

Good morning,

Sorry to leave you like this, but I had to get an early start. You looked so peaceful sleeping that I didn't want to wake you. Thanks for such a wonderful night, and thank you for trusting me.

I'm leaving my home and cell numbers in case you need or just want me. I'll call you.

***

"So, where the hell were you this morning?" Thomas barked when Anthony entered his office. Thomas was a stout man. He stood about five feet six inches, and was just about as wide as he was tall. He was a chain smoker. Although he had tried to give up smoking a few times, he finally resigned himself to the fact that he was a slave to nicotine. He blew his smoke into the air as he stubbed out his cigarette in the glass ashtray on the edge of his desk.

"I had some business to take care of." Anthony took a seat on the leather couch.

"Listen. We can't have you disappearing into thin air. We needed you to be here. We booked the studio for you four hours ago and you didn't even show up." He stood up, walked around to the other side of his desk, and lit up another cigarette. He pulled on it and looked down at Anthony as smoke poured from his nostrils like an angry bull.

"I told you, man. I had some personal business to take care of." Anthony leaned back on the couch and folded his hands behind his head as he stretched out his long legs.

"You're not doing drugs, are you?"

Anthony laughed. "Man, you're crazy. You know I don't touch the stuff. I get high off life, nigga." He leaned forward, rested his elbows on his knees, and clasped his hands. He looked up at Thomas, who towered over him, while he took another puff of his cigarette. "I just got me a little honey, that's all."

Thomas looked up at the ceiling in frustration, then back down at Anthony. "Look, man. You don't need no woman. All of these little hoes running around here after you. Why would you need a woman?"

"I don't want any of those other women. They can't do nothing for me."

"Three months ago they were sucking your dick. Now they can't do nothing for you."

"Man, that shit's over with. I'm in love."

Those were not the words that Thomas wanted to hear.

"Aw, hell no," he said as he put his cigarette out and sat down next to Anthony. "Now, why you want to go and say some shit like that? You don't know nothing about love. It's just lust. The pussy's good. I understand you think you're in love, but man, there's other good pussy around here. Hell, you've had the best pussy in the business."

"Look, man. You don't understand. It's not about sex. I haven't even slept with her. She's just . . . " He looked off into space as he tried to find a word to describe her. "She's just everything—everything I need, everything I want."

Thomas looked at him in disappointment. This nigga was fucked up. He hadn't even gotten the pussy yet, and this girl had his nose wide open. "You ain't fucked her and she got you running around here like this already? What she put on you, roots?"

"Naw, man. She's just a nice girl. She's everything, man. She's perfect." He smiled at the thought of her.

"Listen. She can be everything and perfect and all that good shit. Just don't let her fuck up your career."

"All right, man. I'm straight." Anthony looked at him. "You don't have to worry about me, nigga."

"I better not." Thomas stood up and lit another cigarette. "You and I are a team. Don't fuck me over for some little honey."

"Sure thing, man," Anthony said. He wondered what Randi was doing. "So, what's on the agenda for today?"

Chapter 12

As soon as Randi got off the airplane and entered the airport, she spotted Anthony. He had invited her to Des Moines to meet his parents and attend their thirtieth wedding anniversary party. She had agreed, though she was nervous about meeting his family.

He stood at a window with his hands in his pockets as he watched the airplanes arrive and depart. As if he felt her presence, he turned around when she approached him. He smiled and walked over to meet her.

"Hey, baby." He hugged her. His arms felt good around her. She missed him. They hadn't seen each other in two weeks. He kissed her on the cheek.

He stood back to look at her. Damn, this girl had a hold on him. "How was your flight?" He took her carry-on bag.

"It was a little bumpy." She smiled anxiously.

"You look nervous." He hooked his arm in hers as they started toward baggage claim.

"I am. I don't even know what I'm doing here."

"You're here because I asked you to be here."

"But meeting your family . . . "

"Relax. They won't bite." He chuckled. "Actually, they can't wait to meet you. I told them that you were an aspiring writer/director and now Mom keeps going on and on about it. She used to write when she was younger, which is where I get my skills from."

"Skills," Randi said teasingly. "You've got skills."

"Well, let's put it this way. If it wasn't for my writing, I wouldn't be rapping, then I wouldn't have met you. So yeah,

I say I've got skills." He laughed.

They stood at the carrousel and waited for her luggage.

"I hope you're hungry. Mom cooked this big meal for you."

"That's it." She pointed to her luggage as it came toward them. He grabbed the bag.

"Let me take that." She took the carry-on bag while he carried the other. "Why'd she do that?"

"Do what?"

"Your mom." They turned and headed for the car. "Why'd she cook a big meal for me? I'm already nervous as it is."

"She wants to talk to you. Get a chance to know you before the rest of the family sinks their teeth into you and rips you apart."

Randi raised her eyebrow.

"I'm just kidding." He nudged her. "Relax. You got nothing to worry about. They're gonna love you."

As they continued through the airport, Randi started noticing people staring and pointing at them.

"Randi," Anthony said as he glanced over her shoulder and gripped her luggage tighter.

"Yes," she said as she looked up at him. He wore a worried look on his face. Then she heard an unfamiliar sound.

The sound, however, was very familiar to Anthony. "Are you a good runner?" he asked as he continued to stare over her shoulder.

"Yes, why?" The noise was getting louder and closer. She turned around only to see a herd of screaming fans racing toward them. "Oh my God," Randi whispered. She had never seen anything like it before.

"That's why," Anthony said. "Run!" he yelled as he grabbed her arm to get her moving. She nearly fell down as he pulled her. "Run, Randi!" he yelled.

After getting her footing, she gripped her carry-on and they raced through the airport. Anthony held her hand tightly as they dashed in and around other passengers. His legs were so long that he was practically dragging her along. Randi kept glancing over her shoulder at the crowd of fans that appeared to be growing in size the farther they ran. She didn't know how much longer they would have to run before they could escape his fans, but she knew that her legs couldn't endure much more of this chase.

Anthony was used to the mobs of fans. His long legs gave him a huge advantage over them. However, he knew that Randi was slowing and that if he didn't find refuge soon, he'd have to throw her over his shoulder to keep them moving along. He quickly began to search the area for a safe haven to hide from the fans. Recognizing their dilemma, a quick-thinking airport employee got their attention and signaled them to enter a door marked EMPLOYEES ONLY. Without hesitation, Anthony dragged Randi over to the door and they slipped inside.

Once inside, Randi dropped her bag and slid down against the wall until she was sitting in the floor. She struggled to catch her breath while Anthony and the employee peered outside the door and watched the screaming mob race right past them.

"Thanks, man," Anthony said to the employee as he tried to catch his breath.

"No problem, man. That shit was crazy."

"No shit," he said and squatted down next to Randi. "Baby, are you okay?"

She nodded, still breathing heavily. Although she was in good shape, she had never run so hard in her life.

"You sure?"

"Yeah," she finally managed. "I'm okay." She took a few more swallows of air. "Is it always like this?"

"Not all the time. I guess I should have warned you."

"Yeah." She smiled. "I would have packed lighter."

"I thought I was gonna lose you a few times." He chuckled.

"You and me both." She laughed. "I don't know how you do it."

"Practice, baby." He grabbed her hand and pulled her to her feet. "Now let's get the hell outta here."

With a disguise and help from the employee, Anthony and Randi finally reached the car. He slid down into his seat and looked over at her.

"Are you ready to meet the parents?"

"After that run, I'm pumped for anything."

"Good." He smiled, started the car, and pulled out into traffic.

Randi watched him as he maneuvered the white Lexus coupe through the busy streets. He saw her from the corner of his eye.

"What are you looking at?" he asked, not taking his eyes off the road.

"You."

"Why?"

"Because I can't believe I'm here. I can't believe I'm actually . . . " She hesitated.

"Can't believe you're actually what?"

"I can't believe I'm actually putting my trust in your hands."

That was the next best thing he could have heard from her. He looked at her as he reached for her hand, brought it to his lips, and kissed it.

"Yes, you can trust me," he whispered as he placed her

hand back in her lap. He didn't let it go.

She looked down at their hands entwined and smiled.

It didn't take long for them to reach his parents' house. The impressive two-story brick home with a circular driveway was a present from Anthony. He purchased it for them when he released his first CD.

As he pulled into the driveway and parked, he looked over at Randi. "They're good people."

"Just don't leave my side."

He chuckled. "Mad dogs couldn't drag me away from your side."

Randi wasn't worried about mad dogs. She was worried about being abandoned in a group of strangers.

His mother met them at the door. Anthony looked just like her.

"Mom, this Randi Jacobs. Randi, this is my mom."

"Hello, Mrs. Talbert."

"Hello, Miss Jacobs."

"Just call me Randi."

"Then you call me Sylvia. Mrs. Talbert is my mother-in-law's name." She laughed. "Come on in." She stood back for them to enter and gave Anthony an approving nod.

They went into the living room and sat down. Sylvia gave him a *get out of here* look, but he pretended not to see it.

"I'll bet you're tired from your flight," she said to Randi.

"Just a little." Randi smiled nervously.

"Anthony, don't you have something else to do?"

"No." He knew what his mother was trying to do.

His mother gave him another look, but he acted like he didn't see that one either. Finally, she just came out with it.

"Why don't you leave Randi and me alone so we can get to know each other better?"

"I can't, Mom."

"Anthony Lamar Talbert, if you don't get your narrow behind out of here right now . . . " she said through clenched teeth.

Randi found this amusing. Anthony stood up and looked at Randi. "Sorry, baby. Gotta go."

"Is that all it took for you to abandon me?" Randi laughed.

"She used my full name. When Moms uses the full name, you know she means business."

"Abandon? You're not afraid of me, are you?" Sylvia looked at Randi.

"I'm just nervous."

"Don't worry, dear. I don't bite."

Randi laughed. She felt a little more relaxed. "That's what your son has been telling me ever since I met him."

"He hasn't bitten you yet, has he?" she teased.

"Not yet."

"Let me know if he does." She put her hand on top of Randi's. "Anthony, you go get her bags out of the car and put them in the second bedroom at the top of the stairs."

"Okay, Mom." He shrugged his shoulders at Randi and left.

"So, you really do exist," Randi said to Sylvia.

"What do you mean, child?"

"Well, when I first met your son, I thought he was the product of an evil genius."

She laughed. "Was he that bad?"

"He was that bad."

"And you're with him?" She raised her eyebrow.

"Well, he had to do a whole lot of back pedaling to get

me to this point."

They both laughed.

"Well listen, dear. I set you two up in two different rooms. I hope you don't mind not sleeping together while you're here."

"That's fine, Mrs. Talbert—I mean Sylvia."

"So, you must be very special, Randi. You're the only girlfriend Anthony's ever had, and definitely the only woman he's ever brought home."

Hearing his mother call her Anthony's girlfriend nearly knocked her over. She had never considered the reality that she was his girlfriend. *What else could I be?* she asked herself. She was meeting his parents.

"You're all that boy talks about when we can get him to call," she continued. "I can't get him to shut up about how wonderful you are. I think you're good for him."

"Thank you. I'm crazy about him."

"He says you've been through a great deal of pain." Her eyes softened.

"Yes, ma'am, I have." She was surprised that he had told his mother about her problems. She wondered just how much of her pain he had revealed.

"Well, Anthony's a little wild and a little high strung, but all in all he's a good boy." She smiled as she squeezed Randi's hand then stood up. "Now, come on in the kitchen so I can put you to work."

Randi laughed as she followed his mother. She liked her already.

When they entered the kitchen, Sylvia swatted her husband on the behind as he stood with his head in the refrigerator.

"Hey." He pulled his head up to see who assaulted him and saw Randi. "Was that you being fresh, little girl?" he asked.

Randi smiled. "No, sir."

He stood up all the way, and it became clear that Anthony got his height from him.

"Not before dinner," Sylvia scolded as she checked the pots on the stove.

"She's no fun. I'm fifty-six years old and you would think I wouldn't have to put up with this," he teased. "I'm Paul, Anthony's old man." He closed the refrigerator door and extended his hand to Randi. When she reached to shake it, he pulled hers up to his lips and kissed it.

Like father like son, she thought.

"And you must be the beautiful, funny, ambitious..." He stopped for a second to remember. "Oh yeah, and intelligent Randi Jacobs, to use my son's exact words." He winked at her. "If I was twenty years younger, I'd—"

"You'd still be too old for her. Now, stop flirting with your son's girlfriend." Sylvia poked fun at him. She checked the food in the oven.

Anthony came back downstairs and joined them in the kitchen. "You're not mistreating my guest, are you?"

"If your mother wasn't in here supervising, I'd steal her from you." Paul laughed. "After thirty years of marriage, you'd think she'd let me have some fun."

"After thirty years of marriage, you shouldn't remember what fun is." She pulled the roast out of the oven and placed it on the counter. It smelled delicious.

"Randi, you wash your hands and help me set the table for dinner."

"That's right, Mom. Get her trained for me," Anthony said with a big grin.

Randi and his mother both shot him a glance.

"Sorry." He laughed, holding his hands up in mock

119

surrender. "Come on, old man. Show me that garden you're so proud of," he said to his father. The men left while the women set the table.

"Thirty years. That's a long time to be married," Randi said. She wondered how they made it.

"Well, it wasn't all peaches and cream. Sometimes it got hard, real hard."

"Really?" Randi placed the plates on the table while Sylvia added the silverware.

"Yes, but you have to remember; anything worth having is worth fighting for. And boy, did we have to fight to keep this marriage together."

"You look so happy."

Sylvia stopped what she was doing and looked at Randi. "We are, and one day you will be too." She smiled. "Just be patient. It'll happen."

After dinner, Randi decided to head upstairs to bed. She was tired.

"I'll walk you up." Anthony got up from the table. She followed him upstairs. "So, what do you think?"

"I think they're just as crazy as you are."

"I'll take that as a compliment."

"I like them. They make me feel at home. Now I know where you get all your charm. Your dad is a shameless flirt."

"And proud of it."

They reached her bedroom door. "Here we are," he said.

She turned and looked up at him. His eyes smiled down at her as they stood in silence and gazed at each other.

"I guess I'll see you tomorrow," she finally said.

"I guess you will."

"Good night."

"Good night." He kissed her forehead.

She went into her bedroom and closed the door behind her. Anthony ran back downstairs to see what his parents thought about her. They sat in the den. His father smoked a cigar.

"So, what do you think?" he asked as he entered the room and took a seat next to his mother. He valued their opinion.

"I'd chase after her," his father said between puffs. "She's a good-looking woman."

He looked at his mother. "Mom?"

"I think you did good, son. She's a lovely girl. Thank God you didn't bring one of those hoochie mamas home." She laughed.

"What do you know about hoochie mamas?"

"I see those half-naked women running around in your videos, showing all their stuff and shaking booties all up in your face like they ain't got good sense. Boy, if you brought one of those girls home with you, I would lock both you and her outside."

"I know you would, Mom."

"Randi's a nice girl. You be nice to her." Sylvia knew her son had lots of women after him and that they were tempting. He was young and immature. She knew it would be easy for him to blow this.

"I will, Mom," he promised.

Chapter 13

The next morning, there was a light knock at Randi's door. She sat up in the bed.

Anthony cracked the door open and poked his head inside the room. "Good morning. I didn't wake you, did I?"

"No. Come on in."

He walked over to the edge of her bed and sat down. "How'd you sleep?" he asked

"Good. It's really quiet around here."

"I know. That's because we're so far out in the country."

"It must have been nice growing up here." She climbed out of the bed, walked over to the window and looked out over the land. It was beautiful. Their backyard included a duck pond, a garden, and a small orchard.

"I didn't grow up here. I grew up in a tiny two-bedroom apartment in the middle of the city." He walked over to where she stood. She wore short pink pajamas.

"It's beautiful out here, isn't it?" He looked out the window.

"Yes." She glanced over at him. He was already dressed in a white tank and royal blue shorts. "What time did you get up?" It was only eight o'clock.

"Six o'clock."

"Every morning?"

He sat down on the window seat and looked up at her.

"Yeah, ninety percent of the time."

"Why so early?" She sat down next to him. Her leg rested against his.

"So much to do. Life is too short to sleep it away. You

gotta get up, get out there, and savor every day."

"You sound like a television commercial."

"I know." He chuckled. "Well, it's just you and me today until six. That's the time the party starts."

"Where is everybody?"

"Mom and Dad are putting together a few last minute details and they've got to go get all dolled up for tonight, so they said that we were on our own. You won't meet the rest of the family until we get to the party tonight."

"Then I can go back to bed." She smiled.

"No." He stood up and pulled her to her feet. "Get dressed so we can get out of here. I'm gonna take you to where I grew up at and let you see all the elements that created the man you see standing here before you today."

"Only if you insist on showing me how you became such a mess," she teased.

"I insist. I'll make breakfast, and you can come on down when you're ready."

After he gave her a tour of his old stomping ground, they visited a few of his old friends. They told her stories about him in his Jheri-curl and braces days. To back up the stories, they pulled out photos and embarrassed him even more. Randi doubled over with laughter, tears forming in her eyes.

Anthony sat back and watched as she interacted with them. Her face glowed. She was happy. Suddenly he had an urge to grab her, hold on to her, and steal her away from the rest of the world.

Later, they returned to his parents' home. His parents were not there, but left a note saying that they had already left for the hotel, the party would be in the ballroom, and they

123

would see them there.

Randi and Anthony decided to go ahead and get dressed. Anthony was finished first so he waited downstairs for her. He stood in the living room and flipped through a magazine in his black gabardine and silk Versace suit, looking as if he should be strutting down a runway. Then, as if he felt Randi's presence, he turned around to watch her descend the stairs.

She was breathtaking. Her hair poured down over her shoulders. She wore a little sexy black dress that hugged her body and melted over her curves. Anthony instinctively licked his lips as he went to meet her. He couldn't believe how beautiful she looked.

"You look stunning," he said, unable to take his eyes off her. He took her hand, spun her around to get a better look, and smiled approvingly.

She blushed. "Well, you don't look too bad yourself."

"This old thing?" He pretended to straighten up his suit. "Thank you." He held out his arm for her. "Shall we go, madam?"

"Yes, we shall." She played along and took hold of his arm.

They arrived at the party promptly at 6:00. The ballroom was beautifully decorated in hunter green and gold, the colors his parents used at their wedding thirty years earlier. The colors were everywhere, from the tablecloths to the centerpieces to the balloon arch over the table for the guests of honor.

Beside the dance floor sat the DJ station, a podium where family members and friends could make speeches about the couple, and a fully stocked bar. After dinner, the guests would celebrate with a wedding cake that was an exact replica of the one Anthony's parents had thirty years before.

Rap Superstar

It took Randi a minute to take all this in. She was happy for his parents. They had made it. She wondered how they knew they were soul mates, how they knew they belonged together. She wondered if she and Anthony belonged together. As if he could see what she was thinking, he nudged her, slipped his hand into hers and gently squeezed. She squeezed back as she smiled up at him.

Guests who hadn't seen each other in years stood around socializing and trying to catch up. Through the crowd, Anthony spotted his older brother, who he hadn't seen in almost a year.

"I want you to meet my brother," Anthony said as he led Randi across the room. As they approached Anthony's lookalike, he saw them and grinned.

"Hey, baby brother." He grabbed Anthony and hugged him.

"What's up, man?" Anthony said when he stepped back.

"You, man."

"Yo, Mike, I want to introduce you to my friend." Anthony put his arm around Randi. "Mike, this is Randi Jacobs. Randi, this is my brother, Michael. We call him Mike."

Mike looked at Randi and smiled. "Nice to meet you." He took her hand, brought to his lips, and kissed it. He cut his eyes at Anthony. "Baby brother, you better look out or I'm gonna have to steal her from you." He chuckled.

"Get in line. Dad's already tried but failed miserably."

"That's because he's an old man. He doesn't have the energy it takes to steal a woman like this away." He looked back at Randi. "How'd you end up with this P. Diddy wannabe?"

Randi laughed. "I don't know. I was running. He was

chasing, and he finally caught me." She smiled up at Anthony.

He squeezed her waist. "So, where are Mom and Dad?" he asked as he surveyed the room.

"Anthony. Anthony, is that you?" A plump lady bounded up to him. She grabbed him and hugged him, kissing him on the cheek.

"Aunt Betty," he said when she let go. "How you been?"

"I'm just fine. You look a little thin. Who is this young lady?"

"This is my friend, Randi Jacobs. Randi, this is my Aunt Betty. On my mom's side." Aunt Betty was the Ma Bell of Des Moines. She knew everything, and she told everything she knew.

"My, she's a pretty little thing. But you do need to pick up some weight, dear." She touched Randi's arm then turned back to Anthony. "I'm so glad you're here. Sylvia wasn't sure you were going to make it, you being a big rap star and all. Speaking of rap, I need to talk to about those lyrics. You really should clean that stuff up. Didn't we raise you better than that?"

"Yes, Aunt Betty."

Randi smiled. He sounded like a scolded little boy.

Aunt Betty fidgeted with his suit. "You trying to be like that Puffy man and that Jay something or other. You're a good boy. You don't need to have such a dirty mouth. Promise your Aunt Betty you're gonna clean up your mouth. You're too pretty to have such ugly words coming out of it."

"Yes, Aunt Betty."

Mike and Randi laughed at the way his aunt reprimanded him.

"Can I have your attention?"

They looked in the direction of the podium. The party

coordinator stood at the microphone and announced, "It's time to eat, so if everybody would take their seats, we'll say grace and then you can help yourself to the buffet."

Everyone had assigned seats. Anthony and Randi, along with Mike and Aunt Betty, were assigned to the guests of honor table. When they reached the table, his parents were already seated. Anthony walked over to them, kissed his mother on the cheek, and shook his father's hand.

"I'm proud of you guys," he said. He went back over to Randi and helped her with her seat.

"Thank you," she said as he pushed her chair in behind her.

He sat beside her, and Mike sat on the other side. During dinner, Mike and Anthony caught up on what each was up to. However, Anthony noticed that Mike was more interested in talking to Randi and getting to know her better.

"Randi wants to be a writer," his mother told Mike. He had done a little writing himself.

Anthony watched as Randi and Mike talked. Mike was more suitable for her than he was, he thought. Mike was older, more settled, and hadn't slept with the hundreds of women he had. Mike was ready to settle down, get married, and have children. Anthony hadn't thought about settling down until he met Randi. He knew she was the one, and he didn't intend to let her get away.

After dinner, Sylvia and Paul moved to the front of the room where guests made speeches and presented gifts. Anthony and Mike had to offer words about their parents, and now it was Anthony's turn. He stood up and walked to the podium.

He cleared his throat, smiled at his parents then informed the crowd, "I promise I'm not gonna rap."

Everybody laughed. He caught a glance of Randi. She

127

smiled.

"I've known these two people for over twenty-four years now, but I still find myself speechless when I try to explain what they mean to me and what this day means to them. Being a rapper, I guess that's pretty bad. I'm supposed to be able to freestyle, so while I'm not gonna to rap, I am going to just look at these two people and tell you what I see." He looked at his parents. They held hands.

"When I look at these two people I see love, peace and joy. I see heartache and pain, laughter and tears. I see struggles and overcoming, I see forgiveness and faithfulness. I see respect and adoration. I see wars and surrenders. I see patience, virtue, and happiness. I see mountain peaks and low valleys. Mom and Dad, we all know there can't be peaks without valleys or sunshine without rain. But whatever you've been through, you've made it through. When I look at you, I see a strong and powerful marriage. I see where I want to be one day. So, I must say that I'm proud of you. I love you, and I respect you. And Mom, I have to say that if after thirty years of marriage you can still love this man, then maybe some special lady could learn to love me the same."

He walked over and kissed his parents. Everyone clapped. He glanced at Randi. She looked like she approved of his speech. Maybe one day she could love him, he thought. He made his way back over to her and sat down.

"Did I do good?" he asked.

"You did great." She squeezed his arm.

After the speeches and a few more introductions, the DJ started playing music. He began with Al Wilson's "Show and Tell" at the request of Anthony's parents. They danced the first dance alone. Later, the older guests joined the couple as the DJ played a few more oldies but goodies.

"Do you want something?" Anthony asked before he

ordered himself a drink.

"Water."

"Can I get an Icehouse and bottled water?" he requested. After the bartender brought the drinks, Anthony threw some money in the tip jar.

"Are you having a good time?" he asked as they watched the older folks dancing.

"Yeah. Your family is great, and your Aunt Betty is crazy."

"Every family has one."

"Well, at one point I thought she was going to pull out a switch, make you drop your pants and whip you." She smiled and took a sip of her water.

"It wouldn't be the first time. Aunt Betty got my rear end a whole lot of times. She'd get me, my neighbors would get me, and then they'd call my mom and she'd get me when I got home." He took a swallow of beer.

"You must have been a bad kid."

"I was." He chuckled.

"Who was worse, you or Mike?" She looked up at him. Yeah, he was a bad boy. The one Momma warned her about.

"I was. Mike's always been a good guy. He followed all the rules. Dotted his I's and crossed his T's. Never got in any trouble. Probably a lot like you."

"But you stayed in trouble."

"Yep. Never knew how to avoid it. Trouble just followed me around like a shadow."

Mike walked over to them. "Now, you can't hog this lady all night." He laughed. "Share."

"C'mon, man. I don't see her every day. My time with her is precious. Go harass someone else."

"I'm not harassing you, am I?" Mike asked Randi.

"No." She smiled

"Well, let's go dance." He took her by the arm.

"I really . . . " She looked at Anthony.

"C'mon. He doesn't mind. You don't mind, do you, baby brother?" He took Randi's water and set it on a table.

"If she doesn't mind," Anthony answered.

"Good." Mike pulled Randi onto the dance floor. She looked back at Anthony as if begging for help.

Anthony watched as Randi and Mike danced. She was an excellent dancer. He wasn't thrilled about seeing her dance with another man, even if it was his brother. Mike was still a man and he was single. He was the competition.

Randi's body moved to the music as if it were her natural rhythm, as if the music were her heartbeat. Each step was so precisely executed. She was beautiful, and she moved beautifully. When the music ended, Anthony thought they would stop dancing, but they didn't. They continued on to the next song.

He walked around socializing, trying to ignore what was happening on the dance floor, but Randi had unintentionally caused a scene. Her technique and style of dance made people stop to watch her. She was obviously unaware of her audience as her body devoured the music.

Anthony paused and watched them again. Mike was having too good a time with his woman, and although they never touched during their dance ritual, their bodies spoke to each other.

Anthony went to the bathroom and hoped they'd be finished when he returned. He was disappointed to see them still on the dance floor. His mother caught a glimpse of the worried look on his face and walked over to him.

"Hey, baby" she said. "Is everything okay?"

"Oh yeah, Mom." He forced a smile. He hated to

admit that he was jealous of Randi dancing with his only brother.

Sylvia stood beside him and watched what was happening on the dance floor. "Randi is a good dancer."

"She is."

"You'd better be careful. I think your brother's in love," she teased.

"It looks like it."

"You'd better go and rescue her." She knew that this woman had to be special to have this effect on him. Mike fell in love every six months, but Anthony had never fallen in love before, and she didn't want Randi to get away from him.

"I can't do that. Then I'd look like a fool," Anthony said.

"No. You'd look like a man in love."

"It's that obvious, huh?"

"That obvious. Now go and get her."

Anthony walked across the room to the dance floor and danced behind Randi. She turned around. He placed his hands on her hips as they moved to the rhythm. Mike continued dancing behind her until Sylvia approached him. She slid in between Mike and Randi and danced with him.

Randi liked the way Anthony's body moved. She saw him dancing in the videos, but these movements were different. His hands on her hips made her feel sexy. She held her hands up in the air as he pulled her closer. Their bodies almost touched. She looked up at him and smiled devilishly.

She is so sexy, he thought.

She turned in his hands and pushed her back up against his chest. He felt her behind barely touching his groin as their bodies moved in harmony.

"I didn't know you could move like this," he whispered against her ear.

She turned around to face him. "There's a lot of stuff about me that you don't know."

"How about sharing?"

"Maybe one day."

After a few more songs, the DJ announced that the next song would be the famous Cha-Cha Slide.

"I can't do that." Randi started to leave the dance floor.

"Sure you can. Come on." Anthony pulled her back.

"I don't know how," she insisted.

The music started and the crowd rushed to the dance floor. They started moving.

"Watch me. I'll show you." He moved her out of the way of the other people.

Mike grabbed her other arm. "C'mon, Randi, you can do this."

She watched them and clumsily tried to mimic their movements. The brothers encouraged her until she finally got the routine down. All three of them began to move in synchronized steps. They had a good time.

After the song, Randi sat down while Anthony went to get her some more water. Mike walked with him.

"So, what's the deal with you and Randi?" Mike asked while they stood at the bar and waited for the drinks.

"What do you mean?"

"You introduced her as a friend. What type of relationship do you have with her?"

"She's my girl," he answered after he got his drinks.

"Yeah right."

"She is."

"She's not your type."

"Not my type? What's my type?"

"You know what you're used to. Don't forget you told

me about all those women." They walked over to the side so they could have more privacy.

"I don't mess with those girls anymore," Anthony said.

"Anthony, please. All those women throwing themselves at you and you not hitting it. You used to get head from a different girl every night."

"Man, I've changed. I haven't been with another woman in months. I'm in love, man."

"Love? You crazy. You wouldn't know love if it bit you in the balls."

"For real, Mike. I'm in love with Randi."

"For real?" Mike still didn't believe him.

"You've met her. She's perfect. She's all that I want but more than I deserve. I've got plans for me and that girl."

"And you're serious, baby brother?"

"I'm serious."

"What about her? Is she in love with you?"

"I don't know, man. She's been thrown a few times, and she's afraid to get back up on the horse. Some nigga did some crazy shit to her."

"Once bitten, twice shy, huh?"

"Yep. So I'd appreciate if you'd stop trying to push up on her."

"Okay, but I know you. If you mess up, I'll be right there."

"I ain't trying to mess this up," Anthony told him.

"Well, go do your thing, baby brother."

After a few more songs, the DJ slowed it down with Luther Vandross and Cheryl Lynn singing "If This World Were Mine." Randi was talking to a couple of his cousins when Anthony walked up behind her.

"I want to dance with you," he whispered in her ear. He apologized to his cousins for stealing her away and pulled her over to a corner.

"I thought you wanted to dance."

"I do. Right here. I don't want to know that anybody else is in the room. Just you and me." He pulled her to him. His arms went around her waist, his hands rested on her lower back.

"You be careful with those hands," she teased as she laid her head against his chest. She loved this song, and being there in his arms felt so right.

He pulled her closer as they swayed to the music. She could hear his heartbeat, and although they barely moved, it pounded uncontrollably.

He started to sing so lightly that she could barely hear him, but it didn't matter. He just felt and smelled so good. This was perfect. She looked up at him as he sang to her.

He brought one hand up and held her face. Then he gently rubbed his thumb across her lips. They were so soft, just waiting to be kissed. He caressed her cheek as he tilted her face up to him. He lowered his head and his lips barely grazed hers. When he felt her respond, he kissed her softly and slowly. She parted her lips as she felt his tongue enter her mouth. *She tastes so sweet she could give a nigga a toothache,* he thought. He kissed her deeper as if trying to taste her soul. Randi's arms tightened around him as she held him closer. He dropped tiny kisses on her cheek and chin, before he reluctantly pulled away.

Randi opened her eyes and looked up at him. They stared into each other's eyes.

"What was that for?" she whispered. She still held onto him.

"Because you looked like you needed to be kissed."

"Oh, really?" She raised an eyebrow.

"Really."

"And what does needing to be kissed look like?"

"Like you look right now." He lowered his head and kissed her again.

"Hey, you two. Get a room," Mike said as he approached them. They pulled away from each other and laughed.

"What's up, man?" Anthony asked.

"The Soul Train line has just started. You know you can't miss that."

Anthony looked at Randi. "Shall we?"

"We shall," she replied.

The next morning, Randi got up, showered, and got dressed. After she packed, she went downstairs into the kitchen. Sylvia sat at the table drinking coffee and reading the paper. Anthony and his father piddled around outside in the garden.

"Good morning, sleepy head." Sylvia looked up from her paper. "We saved you some breakfast."

"Thanks." Randi picked up the plate of food they had left for her, and put it in the microwave.

"Did you have a good time last night?" Sylvia asked.

"I did." She stood by the microwave and waited for her food.

"You're going to have to visit us again."

The microwave started beeping.

"I'd like that." She took her food out and sat down at the table with Sylvia.

"I think you're good for Anthony."

"You think so?" She took a bite of her food.

"Yes, I do. You're a nice girl, a good girl; exactly what he needs."

"Anthony's been out there." She took a swallow of water.

"He has. Nevertheless, I think he's met his match in you. I see the way he looks at you. He's a changed man."

"You know he tried to sleep with me the first time we got together," Randi confessed.

"Did you slap the soup out of him?"

"No. But I did run as fast as I could to get away from him," Randi answered between bites of food.

"But he caught you."

Randi thought for a minute. "I guess he did." She stopped smiling.

"Don't look so sad, honey. Falling in love isn't as bad as it seems." She touched Randi's arm as she stood up from the table. "Anthony's not perfect. No one is. I only hope you can appreciate the way he feels about you." She walked over to the sink.

Randi stood up and followed her. "How does he feel about me?" She handed Sylvia her plate.

Sylvia rinsed it off and stuck it in the dishwasher. "He loves you, dear."

"He loves me." She looked at his mother in disbelief.

"Can't you tell?"

Anthony and his father entered the kitchen. "Hey, baby." Anthony kissed Randi's cheek. "Did you sleep well?"

Randi looked at his mother then up at him. "Yeah, did." She forced a smile. Did he really love her like his mother said? Was he feeling the same way that she felt for him? She couldn't think about it now. "Good morning, Paul," she said to his father.

"Good morning, sweetness." He winked at her.

Anthony looked at his watch. "I guess we better get you to the airport. Your plane leaves in about hour and a half."

"I guess you're right."

Anthony went upstairs and got her bags. Randi thanked his parents for a wonderful time and for their hospitality, then Anthony took her to the airport. Her flight would leave at 10:00.

"You didn't say much in the car," he said after they checked her bags. "Is something wrong?"

"No." She smiled as she thought about what his mother had told her.

"Did my mom say something to you?" he asked as he adjusted the ball cap he wore to disguise his identity.

"No, she didn't." She looked into his eyes. "I really had a wonderful time. Thank you for inviting me."

"I hate to let you leave." He pushed some stray hairs back off her face.

"I hate to leave."

"Then don't. Fly with me back to L.A."

"You know I can't do that."

They called her flight number for boarding. She looked around at the gate then back at him.

"How about in two weeks? You can come and stay with me for a couple of days. See what it's like to live in my world."

"It sounds good." She would love to visit him in L.A.

"Good. I can show you around, introduce you to my peeps. I'll even take you to the studio."

"Okay." She agreed

They called her flight number again.

"I've gotta go."

"I know." He pulled her to him, kissed her and hugged her tight. He didn't want to let her go. "I love you," he whispered as he released her.

She stepped back from him, not sure if she believed her ears. She wanted to tell him that she felt the same way, that she had been in love with him for weeks, but she feared that by admitting it, their relationship would move a lot faster than she was ready for. She looked into his eyes then turned and walked away from him. She hadn't said a word, he realized. He had blown it. It was too soon for her.

He watched as her pace slowed and she turned around. She walked back toward him. She didn't care if the relationship was moving too fast. She wanted him to know. She wanted the whole world to know. A tear raced down her face and she quickly wiped it away as she approached him. Her arms went around his neck as she pulled him down to her. His mouth covered hers. She kissed him as if it was the last time. Finally, she pulled away.

"I love you too," she whispered against his lips before completely releasing him. She turned and walked away. This time she did not turn back.

Anthony smiled. She loved him too.

Chapter 14

Two weeks later, Anthony was picking Randi up at LAX airport. "I missed you," he said when met her. He grabbed her in an embrace.

"I missed you too." She stepped back and looked up at him.

A couple of weeks had passed since they last saw each other. She was happy to be there. They collected her bags and headed for his place.

She looked out the window of his pearl white Escalade at the beautiful sights of L.A. She felt his hand on hers and looked over at him. He smiled. He couldn't believe she was actually there.

It wasn't long before they arrived at his apartment. He opened the door to let her inside. Her mouth dropped as she entered the living room. It was huge.

"This is an apartment?" She looked around. "This is bigger than my mom's house."

The room was beautifully decorated. It was simple but elegant, nothing like she would expect from a single man's apartment. The walls were a slate blue, accented by the dark blue drapes pulled open to allow the sunlight in and reveal a spectacular view of the city.

The room, decorated with expensive leather furniture, was complete with a 46-inch television, a fireplace, and a semi-circular bar.

"Anthony, this is beautiful," she told him.

"It's what I call home. Come on. I'll show you to your room, and then you can take a look around." She followed

139

him down the massive hallway.

"I don't usually have company," he said as they passed the first door. "This is my bedroom." They kept walking. "Mom and Dad may come up and stay a day or two with me, so I have a second bedroom." He got to the second door, opened it then stepped back to allow her to enter.

The walls were a rose color. In the middle of the bedroom was a four-poster queen-sized bed covered with a pale yellow comforter decorated with a rose pattern to match the drapes and lampshade. The white furniture gave the room an elegant touch.

"So, did you do all this decorating yourself?" she couldn't help but ask.

"Hardly." He chuckled. "I got my mom to come down and decorate it for me. If I had decorated it then all you would see is black and leather."

"Your mom has good taste."

"She must have. She likes you a lot." He set her bags in a corner. "Go ahead and make yourself comfortable. You can look around if you like. I need to make a couple of telephone calls."

"Okay."

He went back into the living room and got on the telephone while Randi explored the rest of the apartment. She cracked open the door to his bedroom and stuck her head in. She wasn't sure what to expect— maybe whips and chains— but instead, she found another tastefully decorated room. She entered it and admired the décor in comforting shades of green.

A hunter green leather recliner sat near the window. Maybe he liked to sit back and watch women strip for him, Randi thought. She wondered how many women had been guests in his bedroom.

She peeked inside his bathroom. The floor was tile green marble. He had a sunken Jacuzzi tub and a separate glass-enclosed shower. There were his and hers marble sinks and a walk-in closet.

Curious, opened the medicine cabinet. He had all the usual, as well as a box of condoms. She picked up the box and looked at it. *Magnum,* she thought. *So, he's got it like that.* She smiled as she put the box back.

When she returned to the living room, he was just getting off the telephone.

"So, whatcha been doing?" he asked when he saw her.

"Just checking out your place."

He pulled her into his arms. "What do you think?" He pushed her hair back from her face as she looked up at him.

"It's nice. I'm impressed."

"Well, thank you," he said before kissing her. "I've missed you so much, girl."

The telephone rang and he answered it. Randi sat on the couch and waited for him to finish his conversation. After he hung up the telephone, he told her that it was his manager. They had been trying to get some studio time to work on his new album. The studio would be available in half an hour. They had to meet Thomas over there for a couple of hours. He would show her around when they finished.

When they got to the studio, Thomas Day, along with his producers, Irvin Douglas and Warren Martin, were already there.

"This is where it all happens," Anthony said as he opened the door for her. "This is where they make me a star."

The men stood when they saw Randi. Anthony introduced them.

"So, this is the famous Randi Jacobs." Thomas shook her hand. His eyes strolled up and down her body without any shame. "It's nice to meet you."

"Nice to meet you." She pulled her hand away from his. She didn't like the way he leered at her.

"This shouldn't take too long." Anthony kissed her on the forehead. "Go ahead, sit down and relax." He went into the booth while his producers went back to the mixing console and started talking to him.

"Why don't you come over and sit next to me?" Thomas suggested as he patted the space beside him on the couch.

Randi agreed and sat down. She tried to focus on what was going on with Anthony in the recording booth, but something about Thomas made her feel uneasy. In the booth, Irvin gave Anthony a few instructions then he put on his headset. Warren started the music. She liked the beat.

She felt Thomas's eyes on her. "Anthony is a lucky man," he said.

Randi looked at him as he licked his lips and grinned. He reminded her of the Cheshire cat in *Alice in Wonderland*.

"I mean damn, baby. You got your shit together."

"Thank you." She forced a smile. She wasn't sure if he was giving her a compliment or coming on to her. As Anthony started rhyming, she turned her attention back to him and tried to focus on his lyrics.

> *Girl, your ass is wearing them jeans,*
> *Like the skin on a grape,*
> *And though I'm peeping your talent,*
> *Make no mistake.*
> *Brothas sweating you hard,*
> *All up in your area,*
> *'Cause we feelin' you, girl.*
> *Damn, you wifey material.*

You make me wanna settle down,
Get a legitimate gig.
Make me wanna buy a ring,
Have 2.5 kids.
When you step up in the club,
You cause mass hysteria.
Brothas don't know how to act,
'Cause you wifey material.

I see you licking your lips,
And smiling with your eyes.
The swivel in your hips,
Got a nigga hypnotized.
We all trying to see if
We fit your criteria.
No more playas for life,
Shit, you wifey material.

Thomas slid closer to her. "You know I own that boy right there. A sistah like you don't have to settle for the help when you can have the owner," he whispered in her ear. His breath was hot on her face and it stank of cigarettes. "Let me know when you feel like fucking a real man."

"Get lost, you creep," she muttered as she stood up. Anthony looked over at her to see what was wrong. She mouthed the words to him that she would wait for him outside as she pointed to the door. He nodded. She left the room.

Thomas leaned back on the couch with a big grin on his face. *She won't be around here too long*, he thought. Anthony didn't need her in his life. She was bad for both him and his career. His rhymes were getting soft. He was turning into a little punk-ass nigga for this ho who wouldn't even give up the pussy. No, Thomas thought, he wasn't throwing away his golden egg-laying goose just because this trick had his boy's nose wide open. He would do whatever it took to make sure she didn't stick around.

Randi paced in the hallway, wondering what was Thomas's problem, before she decided to venture outside to get some fresh air. The sun seemed hotter in L.A than it was in North Carolina. It beamed down on her skin. A cool breeze came by and gave her a little relief from the heat. After a while, Anthony came searching for her.

"What are you doing out here?"

"Just wanted to get some fresh air." She tried to smile.

"Thomas didn't say anything out of the way to you, did he? He can be an asshole sometimes."

"No," she lied. She didn't want to tell him that Thomas had come on to her. She didn't want to cause any controversy.

"So, what did you think about the new song?"

"I liked it. I didn't hear much of it, but I did like the beat and what I heard of your lyrics."

"Well, we've gotta lay down one more track and then we'll be able to leave. It's hot out here. Why don't you come back inside and get in the air?"

"I will in a minute."

He studied her face. "Are you sure you're okay?"

"I'm fine," she assured him. "Now, go back and finish what you have to do."

"I won't be long," he said before he went back into the building.

Randi went back inside a minute or two later to get out of the heat. She took a sip of water from the fountain and waited in the hallway for Anthony.

Some time later, Anthony and the rest of the guys emerged from the recording room. They were laughing, obviously happy with the results of their work.

"That shit was as tight as hell," Irvin said. "And I'm feeling those lyrics."

"At the rate you're moving, man, we can get that album finished before Christmas," Warren said.

"Well, I'd like to see it drop before then." Thomas looked at Anthony. "If you can give us some more of your time, we can make it happen."

"I'll see what I can do." Anthony walked over to Randi and put his arm around her.

"Check this out," Thomas said. "I'll see you at the pool party today, right?" He looked at Anthony.

"What pool party?"

"Marvin Sadler is having a party today at his place. You were invited. I thought I told you."

"Naw, man. I don't remember anything like that."

"Well, he's working on his new movie. He's considering you for a role, so you gotta be there." He pulled out a cigarette and lit it.

"I got plans with Randi today."

Thomas took a draw off the cigarette. "Bring her. I'm sure she has a bikini." He smiled at her. "You can't miss this opportunity. All the big-name rappers are into the movies now. P Diddy, Ja Rule, DMX, LL, even Bow Wow. You gotta to keep your name out there." He took another draw on his cigarette and blew the smoke up in the air.

Anthony looked down at Randi.

"It's okay," she said.

"Are you sure you don't mind? We don't have to."

"Sure you do." Thomas edged in.

"I don't mind. We're in your world, right?"

He nodded. "We'll just stop by for an hour or two and then we'll have the rest of the day to ourselves." He looked at

Thomas. "What time does it start?"

"Two o' clock."

"You guys gonna to be there?" Anthony asked Irvin and Warren.

"Hell yeah," they said in unison.

"Beautiful women in bikinis, you don't have to twist my arm," Warren said with a smile.

"That's what I'm talking 'bout," Irvin added.

"You know where his place is?" Thomas asked.

"Yeah, I know. I'll be there," Anthony answered

Anthony apologized to Randi as they drove back to his place to get their swimsuits.

"It's all right. This should be nice." She put her hand on his.

Back at his place, Randi put on her bikini and wore it under her shorts and T-shirt. Anthony just wore his swimming trunks and a T-shirt. When they got to Marvin Sadler's place, Randi's mouth dropped open. It was a mansion. She had never seen a place like it in real life, only on television or in the movies. It was a pale yellow, southwestern-style mansion with a red terracotta roof. The circular driveway was packed with luxury cars from Ferraris to Porsches to Jaguars to Bentleys.

People actually live like this in real life, she thought.

Anthony looked over at her and saw the look of astonishment on her face. "Breathtaking, ain't it?"

She looked over at him. "Never in my wildest dreams could I have dreamed up a place like this. I mean, I know that people live like this but I, I . . . " She couldn't find the words to describe it.

"I know," he said. "First time I saw a place like this, it blew my mind to think that one day I could live like this."

Two valets approached and opened their doors. Anthony gave his keys to one of them and walked around to

Randi's side of the car. He took her hand and led her up to the mansion.

The butler opened the massive door and instructed them to follow. Randi looked around at the huge foyer with two spiral staircases that met at the top. The marble floor was so polished they could see their reflections in it. The sunlight danced off a huge crystal chandelier hanging above them.

Randi tried not to look starry-eyed, but she wanted to drink up as much as she could as they walked through the house to the back. The rooms were enormous. Beautiful, one-of-a-kind paintings decorated the walls. Drapes made of fabrics from the most exotic places in the world covered the windows.

When they got to the pool area, Randi was even more taken aback. The place was swarming with beautiful women and men, all dressed in the tiniest swimsuits. There was an Olympic-sized pool where a couple of people played water games. Models lay out in lounge chairs, trying to catch some rays. Off to the side were two square-shaped Jacuzzis filled with people laughing and drinking champagne that came from the bar where the most expensive alcohol flowed like water. Other guests sat beneath huge palm trees that provided shade from the sun, or enjoyed the exotic foods spread out on the enormous buffet table. A DJ entertained them all, pumping out some of the latest and hottest music in the hip-hop industry.

Anthony's arm tightened around her waist. "You want something to drink?" he asked.

"Yeah," she said as she continued to take in the view.

They walked over to the bar where he ordered her some water and himself a glass of champagne. Just as Anthony handed her a bottle of Evian, she spotted Thomas walking toward them. He wore bright orange swimming trunks, shamelessly revealing his hairy back and potbelly. It was so large that Randi hoped there was a doctor around just in case he went into labor.

"You made it," he managed to say with a cigarette wedged between his thin lips.

"Only for an hour or two," Anthony reminded him.

"C'mon. I want you to meet Marvin." He pulled the cigarette from his lips as they followed him. "This could be good for your career."

They approached an older man sitting in a chair with a beautiful woman on his lap. When he saw them, he signaled the girl to get up, then he stood.

Thomas introduced them. "Marvin Sadler, this is Anthony Talbert, a.k.a. Animalistic. Anthony, this is Marvin Sadler."

Anthony removed his arm from Randi's waist and shook Marvin's hand. "This is my lady, Randi Jacobs."

Marvin shook her hand then turned his attention back to Anthony. "I'm interested in putting you in my latest movie."

"Why don't you two talk shop and I'll entertain Randi here?" Thomas offered as he gave her one of his wicked smiles.

"That's okay," Randi said. "I'll be all right on my own."

"You sure? Thomas can keep you company." Anthony didn't want her to feel stranded.

"I'm sure," she answered, trying to avoid Thomas's gaze.

Anthony leaned down and kissed her. "I won't be too long."

"Okay." She walked over to the one of the lounge chairs by the pool and sat. Anthony sat down with Marvin to discuss the movie, but kept his eyes on her.

Randi took a couple sips of water as she watched the people in the pool play volleyball. She got splashed a couple of times and the water felt good. A few minutes later, she decided to take a dip in the pool to escape the heat. She slipped off her sandals and stood. She pulled off her T-shirt, unfastened her shorts and let them fall to her ankles to reveal a sexy little black bikini.

Damn, Anthony said to himself when he saw this. He no longer heard what Marvin was saying.

She picked up her clothes, folded them, and laid them on her chair. When she started to get into the pool, one of the guys who was already in swam over to help her.

"Thanks." She took his hand and lowered herself into the cool water. Anthony watched intensely.

The stranger introduced himself. "My name is David Daniels."

"Randi Jacobs."

"Are you new? I haven't seen you around at any of these parties before."

"I'm not in the business. I'm just here with my friend."

"So, this friend of yours, male or female?" he asked.

"Male." She smiled.

Marvin finally got Anthony's attention. "I've got a script that you can take home, read, and then you can call me with your thoughts."

"That sounds good," Anthony answered, eyes still glued to Randi and her new friend. Marvin realized that Anthony's mind was elsewhere.

"Go ahead and have fun. I'll have one of my people give you the script before you leave."

"Thanks." They stood up and shook hands.

Anthony walked over to the side of the pool. Randi had gotten rid of her friend and was swimming by herself. He slipped off his shoes and pulled off his shirt. Just as he was about to get into the water, a beautiful model approached him. Randi emerged from below the water and watched them.

"I just love you, Animalistic," the model said. "I've got all your CDs. You're so damn hot." She pursed her red lips.

"Thank you," Anthony said.

"I'm trying to get into this movie. Maybe we'll be working together."

"Maybe."

She touched his chest with her matching red fingertips. He stepped back from her. "I don't think that's a good idea," he said.

"Well, can a sistah at least get a hug? I'm harmless." She smiled seductively.

He could tell by the devilish smile on her face that she was far from harmless. *Dangerous* was a more appropriate adjective to describe her.

"I don't think that's a good idea either." He had never turned down so many women since he met Randi.

He lowered himself into the water and waded over to her. The model looked at Randi and rolled her eyes before she walked away.

He put his hands on Randi's hips. "I love your bikini."

"You don't think it's too much?" She rested her hands on his arms and looked up at him.

More like too little, he thought. "No," he said. "It looks great on you. It really shows off your—"

"Don't say it." She smiled. "So, how did it go with Marvin?"

"Good. He's gonna give me a script to read so I can see what I think about it. You having fun?"

"Yeah."

He looked over at the Jacuzzis. One of them was unoccupied. "Let's get in the hot tub," he suggested.

They climbed out of the pool and headed the tub. Jason Novice, a video director, stopped them.

"Hey, Anthony, who's this?"

"This is Randi Jacobs. Randi, this is Jason Novice. He's only the hottest video director in L.A."

"Check this out, Randi. I've been watching you. Do you do videos?"

Randi was flattered. "No." She smiled.

"Well, I'd be interested in putting you in a few of my videos. What do you think?"

She looked up at Anthony, and before she could answer, he spoke up. "Randi's not interested in doing any videos."

"Let the lady speak for herself," Jason protested.

"I may be interested," she said just to get under Anthony's collar for speaking for her.

"Randi, you're not interested in anything like that," he said.

"Here's my card," said Jason. Randi took it. "Give me a call tomorrow."

"I'll get with you later," Jason said to Anthony before he walked off.

"You aren't really serious about that, are you?" he asked as they went back to the Jacuzzi and climbed in.

"Why not?" She sat between his legs and felt him slip his arms around her waist. His hands rested on her stomach.

"I just don't picture you as a video girl, that's all." Two of his fingers circled her belly button.

151

"Would you protest if I did it?" She rested her elbows on his thighs.

"No. I couldn't. I'd have to respect what you want to do."

She liked his response.

He leaned over and kissed her on the jaw. The fingers on her belly button had started to cause a stir inside her. She parted her legs slightly as if giving him an invitation. As she laid her head back against his chest, she closed her eyes. The thumping sound of 50 Cent's "Twenty-one Questions" pumped through the air.

"I wouldn't do it anyway," she said.

"I thought you said you were interested in it."

"That was just to get your goat since you spoke up for me so fast." She smiled.

"Get my goat?"

"It's an old country saying that means to bother you, get under your skin."

"You're already under my skin." He kissed her ear and gently tugged on it with his teeth.

Her heartbeat quickened as she felt one of his hands drop below her navel. His fingers brushed against the edge of her bikini bottom and played with the elastic band as he gently massaged her belly. He wondered what her response would be if he slipped his fingers down into her bikini. She felt him become aroused as his manhood began to press against her back.

He pulled her tighter against him as his fingers continued to debate whether it was all right to travel even farther down. She opened her legs a little wider and he saw this as an invitation. He slowly slipped his fingers below the waistband and waited for her to stop him. When she didn't, he edged his finger a little farther. He felt the curly hairs of her pubic area. He hadn't touched a woman like that in so long it was ridiculous.

She let out a little moan. It had been a year and a half since someone had gotten this far with her. He inched his fingers down as he thought about her poem and licked his lips. His tongue craved to taste her caramel folds of womanhood.

"What are you two kids up to?" Thomas asked as he walked over to them.

They both jumped, startled back into reality. Anthony quickly pulled his fingers out of her bikini bottom and she automatically closed her legs. Thomas puffed on a cigarette.

"How can you smoke those things in this heat?" Anthony tried to sound calm.

"Can't help myself." He kicked off his sandals. "Mind if I join you?" he asked. Without waiting for a response, he lowered himself into the water directly across from them and started talking about business.

Randi closed her eyes again and laid her head against Anthony's chest. He had lost his erection. The vibration of his voice made her doze off.

"Little lady's not used to this lifestyle," Thomas joked.

A short while later, Thomas left and Anthony awakened Randi. Drowsily, she looked up at him. He kissed her temple.

"You ready to get out of here, baby?" he asked.

"Yeah."

They climbed out of the Jacuzzi and found some towels on a nearby table. After drying themselves, they slipped back into their clothes. Before they left, Anthony caught up with Marvin and got the script he promised. Because Randi was tired from the jetlag and the hot sun, they picked up some takeout, rented a couple of movies, and headed back to his apartment.

After a shower and dinner, they lay on the couch together and watched the movies. Within a few minutes, they both fell asleep.

Hours later, Anthony woke up. Since Randi was still asleep, he decided to put her in bed. He carefully slid from behind her and climbed off the couch, trying not to wake her. Gently, he picked her up in his arms and carried her down the hall to her bedroom. He attempted to lay her down without waking her, but he wasn't successful.

Her eyes opened as he lowered her onto the bed. Her arm instinctively went around his neck to keep herself from falling. When he laid her down, she didn't let go, forcing him to remain leaning over her. His face was so close to hers that she felt his warm breath on her skin. He looked into her eyes when he realized she wasn't letting go. She stared back, not sure of what she was doing.

Seconds, which seemed like minutes, passed before he slowly lowered his mouth onto hers. He kissed her gently at first, as if he were savoring her lips. When he felt her respond to him, he kissed her deeper. He pushed her lips apart with his own as his tongue entered her mouth. She felt the weight of his body lower down onto hers as he lay on top of her.

She kissed him as she drank from his soul. Her hands moved over his back and she arched her body against his. He brought his hands up to her face and held it as his mouth traveled down to her chin then along her jaw-line then to her neck. She felt the hardness of his manhood against her thigh as he pushed himself up against her. They both wanted more. Finally, he raised his head and looked down at her.

"Can I make love to you?" he asked with his lips barely touching hers. His eyes probed hers for an answer.

She stared up at him. "Yes," she whispered.

"Are you sure?"

"Yes. I'm sure."

He hesitated for a moment. "Wait right here," he said before he kissed her again and got up. He left the room, returning a few seconds later.

Randi was puzzled by this until she saw him lay a condom on the nightstand. He climbed back onto the bed and gathered her in his arms. Slowly he peeled away her clothes, replacing them with long, hot kisses until she lay naked in front of him. He continued to explore her body with his hands and mouth. She arched her back as she felt his mouth cover her breasts. He nursed gently on them before his lips traveled down over her ribs and belly. He paused at her belly button, his tongue probing her flesh while his fingers gently teased her ribs.

When he started moving below her belly button, she protested "Don't." She barely whispered. No one had ever done that to her before.

He raised his head to look at her. She stared back. He gently spread her legs and lowered his head. He heard her gasp as he tasted her with his tongue. He never imagined that she would taste so sweet. *Caramel* was not the word to describe her sugary insides. She closed her eyes. Her hands slowly slid down to his head as her body began to move against his mouth. She felt his tongue entering her, teasing her, driving her crazy. His skilled tongue worked with perfect precision, tasting every crevice of her treasure. She moaned against her will as his mouth continued to savor her sweetness. Then she felt him insert his finger as he continued to tantalize her with his tongue.

"Oh God," she whispered as he inserted another and gently worked it in and out of her.

He felt her legs begin to tremble as she clutched at his head. He pressed his tongue against her clitoris as her body

155

shook uncontrollably. When he felt her go limp, he raised his head and gazed down at her beautiful body.

He stood up, removed his clothes and released his swollen manhood, which had been straining against his pants. He reached for the condom and slipped it on without taking his eyes off her. Slowly, he climbed between her opened legs and lowered himself on top of her.

She felt his hardness pressing against the inside of her thigh. He kissed her gently, sliding one hand down to her thigh and spreading her legs open wider. As he began to enter her, he felt her body tense up against the pain.

"Are you okay?" He looked into her eyes.

She nodded as she tried to relax. He pushed himself all the way inside her.

"Damn," he whispered. "You feel so damn good."

She felt herself opening up around him. He waited patiently for her body to relax and accommodate him. Slowly, he began to move against her as his mouth traveled from hers down her jaw then to her neck. He moaned as her body responded to his.

Although he had slept with hundreds of women, nobody ever made him feel like he felt with Randi. They moved in a slow, rhythmic motion together. Their pace quickened as their passion built. Her fingers clutched at his back as she reached another climax. His body became tense as he drove himself deeper and deeper inside of her. He held her as if he was holding on for life.

"Oh God." He moaned. "Oh God, Randi." His entire body became rigid as he shuddered. She held him tightly as he collapsed on top of her. Gently, she stroked his head as he lay exhausted. His breathing began to calm down as he pulled his fingers through her hair.

"I love you so much, Randi." he managed to whisper

against her ear. He raised his head up and kissed her deeply.

"I love you too," she whispered as she looked into his eyes.

He rolled off her and pulled her into his arms. After he pushed her hair away from her face so he could see her, he tilted her head up and forced her to look him in the eyes.

"I'm going to make you happy," he promised.

"You already have."

He pulled her face to his and kissed her as he caressed her cheek. She lay her head on his chest. As he fell asleep, she lay in his arms and listened to him breathing. She closed her eyes and felt his heartbeat. Before she fell asleep, she thought, *I hope this wasn't a mistake.*

Later that night, she awakened to an empty bed. She looked over at the glowing numbers of the alarm clock. It was 3:35 in the morning. She wondered where Anthony was. After lying in the dark for a couple of minutes, she pulled on her robe and went to look for him. She found him in his bedroom, sitting on his bed, playing video games on his PlayStation II. He looked like a little boy as he focused intensely on the game.

"You want some company?" she asked as she stood in the doorway.

He looked over at her. "I didn't mean to wake you. Come on in."

"You didn't." She walked over to the bed.

"I couldn't sleep," he explained. "You want to play?"

"I don't know how." She sat on the bed next to him.

"No, come here." He took her hand and pulled her around to sit between his legs. He put the controller in her hands and instructed her. After he pulled her hair back and kissed her neck, he watched her play.

He wasn't going to blow this, he thought. He wasn't

going to let Randi Jacobs out of his life.

When Anthony awakened later that morning, Randi was standing in front of the window, looking out over the city. Still naked, he climbed out of bed, slid up behind her, and slipped his arms around her waist. He kissed the back of her head.

"What are you thinking about?" he asked with his face in her perfumed hair.

"I've got to leave today," she whispered sadly.

He inched her robe down, revealing a little bit of her shoulder, and replaced it with a kiss. "You don't have to. You could stay."

"I can't." She felt his fingers pull her robe open as his tongue traced from her shoulder up to her neck. One of his hands traveled across her belly up to her breasts. He teased the nipple with his fingers.

"Why can't you?" he asked as he gently bit her ear before his tongue darted inside. His hand slid down between her legs and his fingers delicately probed the folds of her womanhood until he felt her moistness.

What is he doing to me? Randi thought as she felt his finger inside of her. Her legs became weak. She needed him.

"Why can't you stay with me?" He asked as his tongue continued to explore her ear.

"I can't."

He turned her around, cupped her face in his hands and kissed her feverishly. Next he slipped the robe all the way off her shoulders and let it fall to her feet. He picked her up, wrapped her legs around his waist, and carried her to the bed. Slowly, he laid her down and allowed his body to rest on top of hers.

"Open your eyes, Randi," he whispered against her lips. She did. He wanted her to see who was making love to her.

They didn't say much in the car on the way to the airport. Anthony kept looking over at Randi as she stared out the window. He didn't want her to leave. They checked her bags then sat down and waited for her flight. She rested her head on his chest and closed her eyes. She tried to remember everything that had happened that weekend. She didn't want to forget any second of it. Well, maybe she could discard the parts containing Thomas.

His hand moved up and down her back in an attempt to make her feel better. His schedule would start becoming hectic for the next few weeks, with the work he had to do on his new album and the movie role he was considering. He didn't know when he would get some free time to see her.

They called her flight number for boarding. She hesitated then stood up. He stood up and pulled her into his arms.

"You don't have to leave, Randi. You can stay here with me," he whispered against her hair. He held onto her, not wanting to let her go. Inside of him, it felt as if his heart was being crushed.

They called her flight number again.

"I have to go," she murmured against his chest.

He still didn't let her go. Instead, he squeezed her even tighter as she sobbed against him. He stroked her hair.

"You don't have to go, baby."

"I have to go." She pulled away from him. He wiped the tears from her face.

"Don't cry." He kissed her eyes, her nose, and her cheek until he found her mouth, where he stayed and drank from her. "I love you," he whispered

159

"I love you." She pulled herself out of his arms, turned around, and walked away without looking back. She knew that if she had, she wouldn't have been able to leave.

Anthony watched as she gave her ticket to the attendant and walked into the tunnel that led to her plane. He sat down in one of the chairs and wiped his eyes.

This was hard, he thought. Love wasn't supposed to make him feel like this.

Chapter 15

"You whore," Kathy said playfully when Randi told her that she had slept with Anthony. "Was it good?"

"It was nice." She tried not to sound too whorish.

"How do you feel about the situation now? Do you think you can handle it?"

"I don't know. It was so hard saying goodbye to him yesterday. I do love him, and he says he loves me. I just hate being away from him."

"Girl, you've got it bad."

"Don't I know it."

"So, when are you going to see him again?"

"I don't know. He's got a pretty busy schedule for the next few weeks. He's going to try to fit me in."

"Well, I'm happy for you. He's the one, Randi. I can tell."

"How can you tell?"

"Because you gave him the bootie." Kathy laughed. She was so happy that her friend had fallen in love.

***

Anthony stood in the studio booth with a headset on. He listened to the beat and tried to focus on the task at hand. However, his mind would slip back to Randi and how good she felt, how good it felt when she put her fingers on his skin, how sweet she tasted. He remembered how her eyes lit up when she looked up at him, how her legs felt wrapped around his waist, and how his heart ached when she walked away

Debra Clayton

from him at the airport.

Talking to her every day was not enough. He wanted to see her and hold her and kiss her. He wanted to make love to her in every way. He was so engrossed in thought he missed his cue to start rapping for the third time in a row.

"What the fuck are you doing?" Thomas barked as he ripped his cigarette out of his mouth. "Get your shit together, nigga."

Anthony ignored his outburst and kept his eyes on Irvin and Warren. "Give it to me again," he said.

They started the music. He nodded his head to the beat and licked his lips. He hit his cue this time and spit out the lyrics, but they were not raw enough for Thomas.

"Hold up, hold up!" Thomas yelled. The music stopped. "Get that bitch out of your head and do your damn job."

Anthony ripped the headset off and pointed at Thomas. "Fuck you, nigga. Fuck you!" he shouted as he paced the floor of the booth. He threw the headset against the wall and tore open the door. "I'm outta here."

Irvin hurried over to him. "He didn't mean nothing by it, dawg. Calm down." He put his hand on Anthony's shoulder to stop him from leaving.

Anthony looked over at Thomas, who calmly pulled on his cigarette and blew the smoke up into the air.

"Sorry, dawg. I was out of line." He took another puff on his cigarette before putting it out in an ashtray. "I know you're in love, man, but you can't let that fuck up your career. We've been doing this shit for over six years now. Don't fuckin' throw it away."

Anthony took a deep breath and exhaled.

"Let's finish this so we can get the hell out of here," Irvin suggested.

162

"All right, man," Anthony agreed and returned to the booth. He got another headset and waited for his cue. This time, he started rhyming the way Thomas wanted him to rhyme.

***

A few days later, Randi pulled up to her apartment building at 11:35 at night. She had just gotten home from work. Slowly, she climbed the stairs to her apartment. She was tired. When she turned the corner, she noticed someone sitting on the porch outside her front door. She hesitated.

The first person she thought of was Eric, and her heart began to thump against her chest. She gripped the edge of the handrail and prepared herself to run. But as the person stood, his face got closer to the porch light, and she realized that the stranger was Anthony. She let out a sigh of relief as she tried to calm herself down.

He walked toward her and pulled a bouquet of white roses from behind his back. He presented them to her.

"What are you doing here?" she asked excitedly.

"So many questions." He laughed as he scooped her up in his arms and kissed her.

They could barely get inside the apartment before they had ripped each other's clothes off. He picked her up, carried her into the kitchen and sat her on the table. He pushed her down until she lay on her back, then he spread her legs. His mouth covered her womanhood as he savored the taste of her warm flesh. Randi closed her eyes as his full, strong lips and agile, skilled tongue took her to ecstasy. After she climaxed, he entered her. He closed his eyes as he felt the warm wetness of her body envelope him. Slowly, gently he made love to her. He gripped her hips as he buried himself deeper.

"Damn, Randi, what the hell are you doing to me?" he moaned just before he spilled himself inside of her. Nearly spent, he picked her up and carried her to the bedroom, where he made love to her again.

A while later, all of his energy was drained and she lay on top of him. His long fingers gently traced up and down her buttocks. He loved the way they fit in his hands.

"Randi."

She lifted her head and looked at him. "Yes."

"I don't like your hours."

"What do you mean?"

"I don't like you coming home this late at night. Like tonight, for example. I could have been anybody. What would you have done if I had tried to attack you?"

"Run, scream, I guess."

He pushed his hand through her hair. "It's not safe." He hated the thought of losing her to some craziness.

"I know, but what else can I do? The earliest I can get off is ten."

"You could quit. Let me take care of you. I think I make enough money." He smiled.

"I'm sure you do, but I can't."

"You can't take money from me?"

"No, I can't."

"Independent woman," he said as he continued stroking her hair. "If you and I were married, you'd still insist on working?"

"I don't know." She changed the subject. "How long can you stay?"

"I've got to leave first thing in the morning. Thomas is already biting my head off for being over here now."

"You like him?" she asked.

"He's all right. He brought me a long way. I owe him a lot."

"No. Your talent brought you a long way. He owes you a lot."

"Getting back to your work schedule, what are we gonna do about it?"

"I don't know."

"Can you get another job? Somewhere you don't have to come home so late at night."

"I like my job. Besides, if it wasn't for that job, I wouldn't have met you."

"Score one for the job."

Chapter 16

A few weeks later Randi was back in L.A. with Anthony. She sat in his car with a blindfold over her eyes as he drove. He had a surprise planned for her.

"Where are we going?" she asked. She felt silly riding around with a blindfold.

"You'll see when we get there. Be patient." He put one of his hands on hers.

She felt good about their relationship. When they were apart, she was a little worried about the distance that separated them, but his daily telephone calls assured her that they would be okay.

After they drove for about thirty minutes, she felt the car slow down, turn off the road and stop. She heard a buzzing sound then the car began to move again, but this time much slower.

"I hope you're not trying to kidnap me," she teased.

"I am." The car stopped again. "We're here," he announced as he got out and walked over to her side. He took her hand and helped her out. She heard the car door shut behind her. He held onto her arm and guided her. After a few more steps, they stopped.

"Are you ready?" He moved behind her.

"Yes." She could barely stand it.

He loosened the blindfold then stopped. "I don't think you're ready," he whispered in her ear.

"Anthony," she scolded.

He removed the blindfold and she opened her eyes. In front of her stood a beautiful, 10,000 square foot, $2.9-million brick mansion. Her mouth fell open as she looked at the house then looked up at him.

166

"So, what do you think?" He squeezed her hand.

"It's beautiful." She looked back at the mansion. "What are we doing here? Are you buying this?"

"Come on." He took her hand and they walked up to the mansion. He removed a key from his pocket and unlocked the door. They stepped inside.

"Oh my God," she said as she looked around.

The foyer was massive, with a beautiful custom-designed hardwood floor and an exquisite chandelier.

"Could you live in a place like this?" he asked as he watched her reaction.

She looked at him in disbelief. "What have you done?"

"Come on and let me show you around." He gave her the grand tour of the six bedrooms, four and a half bath mansion, describing every room to her. There was even a kidney-shaped pool, a sauna for twelve, a tennis court and basketball court.

"This is where we'll be able to watch movies," he said as he showed her the media room. He picked up a remote control from the wet bar and pushed a button. A huge movie screen descended from the ceiling.

"Tell me what's going on."

"Not yet." He led her up the spiral staircase. "This is the master bedroom. Check out the view. "This house sits on twelve acres of land," he continued, sounding like a tour guide. "It has an orchard and a manmade pond."

She walked over to the window and looked out. The landscape was beautifully manicured. She could see the pool, the tennis courts, along with a pond and a detached four-car garage. She couldn't believe this place. He stood behind her with his arms wrapped around her waist.

"Do you like it?" he asked.

She turned in his arms to face him. "Yes, I do," she

167

answered, still confused. "Are you buying this place?"

"Yes." He finally answered one of her questions. "For you." He reached into his pocket and pulled out a small ring box as he got down on one knee in front of her. He took her hand and cleared his throat. Randi put her free hand over her mouth in disbelief and started crying.

"Randi, you're everything to me. When you're away from me, I go crazy. When you're with me, I am weak. I never imagined being in love, much less loving someone the way I love you. I can't picture myself without you. I know this is quick and we've only been together for about three months, but I know that you're the one for me. Baby, you make me want to be a better man. You're all that I want and more than I deserve." He paused. "Will you marry me?"

By the time he finished, Randi was sobbing uncontrollably. He nervously fumbled with the ring box as he opened it and took out the platinum princess-cut three stone diamond ring. He slipped it on her trembling finger and waited for an answer, but she couldn't stop crying. She was in shock and couldn't believe this was happening. She didn't know what to say. He stood up and held her tear-covered face in his hands, tilting her head up forcing her to look at him.

"I don't know what to say." She finally managed to speak.

"Say yes," he said.

"But . . ."

"You love me, don't you?"

She nodded.

"And I love you."

"We . . ."

He brushed the tears from her cheeks with his thumbs. "I can't stand being away from you. You can quit your job, move here with me and I'll take care of you. You won't have to work. You can go to UCLA, take your writing classes and become a famous writer. All you have to do is say yes."

"This so sudden." Her heart pounded.

"If I ask you a year from now, would you say yes?"

"Yes."

He lowered his forehead until it touched hers. "Then all you have to do is say yes now."

"Yes," she whispered.

"Yes?"

"Yes." She nodded as she began to cry even more. "Yes. Yes. Yes."

He rained kisses all over her tear-soaked face before his mouth landed on hers. She could taste her own salty tears from his lips. Their kiss deepened as he crushed her body against his. He slowly pulled away from her.

"There's something else." He took her hand and led her downstairs.

Randi wiped the tears from her eyes. What more could it be? He led her to the garage and opened the door. They stepped inside. In front of her sat a silver Jaguar.

Randi's mouth dropped open. "No." She whispered.

"Yes," he answered as he watched her.

"Anthony!" she cried.

He pulled out the keys and attempted to hand them to her. She just stared at them. He placed them in her hand. "Why don't you take me for a ride?" He opened the car door for her.

Chapter 17

After the initial shock, Kathy agreed to be her maid of honor. They were married six months later on the grounds of their new home.

Initially, Randi's parents weren't pleased with both the facts that they got married so soon and that she married a rapper. However, after they got to know Anthony, they realized that their love was genuine and he wasn't the bad guy they saw in his videos.

On the other hand, Anthony's parents were thrilled from the start. They adored Randi and thought that she was perfect for him.

Anthony had arranged to fly Randi's guests over and set them up in hotels. All of his friends and family were there, including his manager.

Thomas told Anthony that he thought the marriage was a mistake. He told Anthony that although he liked Randi, she made him soft and his music had suffered because of her.

The guest list included some of the biggest names in the business. Uninvited guest included die-hard fans and the paparazzi. Some sneaked in by pretending to be the wait staff for the reception, while others scaled the fence that surrounded their estate. Security caught most of them and escorted them out.

At the reception, Cristal flowed like water. Anthony spared no expense in making sure that Randi had the best of everything. He even arranged for Michael Daniels, Randi's favorite R&B singer, to perform for her. Before the night was over, the infamous Cha-Cha Slide was played, and everybody got up and danced. This time Randi knew the steps.

After the reception, Randi and Anthony said goodbye to their family and friends. They slipped away from their guests in a stretch limousine and made their way to the airport. From there, they boarded a private jet and headed for their honeymoon in the Bahamas.

Two weeks later they returned home. Randi immediately enrolled in classes at UCLA where she majored in creative writing, while Anthony left for a two-month tour. Thomas threw it together at the last minute. Anthony only had two weeks to spend with his bride in their new home before he had to take off.

Randi was a little disappointed that he had to leave so soon, but she understood. She was married to a rap superstar. He was in demand. He couldn't just sit at home babysitting her. Still, she felt that Thomas had set up the tour on purpose. She knew that he wasn't her biggest fan, so she tried not to complain or cause problems between him and Anthony.

While on tour, Anthony managed to call every night to make sure she was fine and to let her know what he was up to. He said that the tour was great, and that every show had been sold out. He promised to be home as soon as he could.

A couple of times, he flew Kathy over to spend some time with Randi. Anthony gave Randi a few credit cards so she could start decorating the mansion. During Kathy's visits, they would spend the day shopping. Kathy made her laugh. And when Randi felt down about Anthony being away, Kathy constantly reminded her of how much he loved her, how much he needed her, and he was only doing his job.

Anthony had a hard time dealing with being away from her also. He rolled over in his bed to reach for her, but she wasn't there. He held on to the memories of what she smelled like, what she tasted like, and how she felt. He carried her picture in his wallet so he could remember her smile.

While all the other rappers were out at after-parties, he was up in his hotel room on the telephone with Randi, discussing the events of their day. He didn't tell her about the women because he didn't want to add to her insecurities.

The women were relentless. They didn't care that he was married. They continued to throw themselves at him. While some stowed away on his tour bus, others attempted to sneak into his hotel room to seduce him. They offered him everything from blow-jobs to anal sex to some of the freakiest things he had ever heard of. Although tempted, he remained faithful to Randi. He knew that even though these women offered him the time of his life, he had his platinum princess at home. He wasn't willing to throw that away for anything or anybody.

***

The hot, steamy water raced down Randi's naked body as she stood in the shower and rinsed her hair. Anthony would be home in two weeks, she thought happily. She couldn't wait to see him. Living off telephone calls for the last month and a half was unbearable.

She hummed a little tune that she had heard earlier that day and couldn't get out of her head. All of a sudden, the shower door opened and there stood Anthony. At first, Randi just stared at him in disbelief. Still fully dressed, he stepped into the shower and pulled her into his arms. He kissed her feverishly and began to remove his clothes. She helped him. Once he was naked, he pushed her back against the shower wall. His hands slipped down to her hips and picked her up. He opened her legs, wrapped them around his waist, and entered her slowly. Her hands clenched at his back. An involuntary moan escaped her lips, and he began to move in that old, familiar rhythm that she loved.

"I've missed you so damn much," he whispered against her ear. He drove himself deeper and deeper inside of her until they climaxed and collapsed in each other's arms.

Afterwards, he carried her to the bedroom where he made love to her over and over again until they were exhausted. Randi held onto him the entire night. She didn't dare let him go.

The next morning, he took her again. He could not get enough of her. As they lay in the bed enjoying the afterglow of their lovemaking, the telephone rang.

"Hello?" Anthony answered.

It was Thomas and he was furious. "What in the hell do you think you're doing?" he barked. He was so loud that even Randi could hear him.

"I'm enjoying my wife's company." Anthony smiled as he looked over at her.

"You owe me two more weeks!"

"I don't owe you shit." He reached over and gently squeezed her thigh.

"You're a fucking pussy, you know that? Now you're gonna to take your black ass back on the road and finish your tour!"

"No. What I'm gonna to do is make love to my wife one more time before I get up and cook her breakfast." He hung up the receiver and pulled Randi into his arms.

Chapter 18

During the next year, Anthony was only away from home a couple of days at a time. He refused to leave Randi for an extended period. Whenever she was out of school, he took her on the road with him.

Randi knew that the friction between Anthony and Thomas was building. They argued a lot about his schedule, and about what he was and wasn't going to do.

"You're throwing away everything we worked for, for this bitch." She overheard Thomas tell this to Anthony.

Anthony stormed out of the room and refused to talk to Thomas for a couple of weeks. Numerous times, Thomas tried to apologize, but Anthony wouldn't accept it. Anthony told Randi that when his contract was up, he was dropping Thomas and moving on. He only had two years left.

Thomas tried to smooth things over with Anthony by inviting him and Randi to a party at his place. Randi didn't feel well that night. She had an upset stomach, so she stayed home. She urged Anthony to go and work things out with Thomas. She felt guilty because she knew that she was the source of all of their disagreements. Reluctantly, he agreed to attend, but insisted that she call him on his cell if she needed anything.

"Kathy, I just took a pregnancy test," Randi blurted out later that night as soon as Kathy answered the telephone.

"What?" Kathy asked.

"I just took a pregnancy test. I've been sick for a few days now and I'm two weeks late." She was excited. "So, I bought this test today and I just took it."

"Are you pregnant?"

"I don't know. I'm waiting for the results. I just didn't want to do it by myself."

"How much longer?"

"Thirty seconds."

After thirty seconds, Kathy said. "Well, don't keep me waiting. What does it say?"

"I'm pregnant!" Randi squealed. "I'm pregnant." She jumped up and down.

Kathy joined in the squealing.

"Are you ready for a baby?" Kathy asked after they calmed down.

"Yes."

"What about Anthony? Do you think he's ready?"

"I don't know. I know he wants kids, but Thomas is giving him a hard time about me. A baby right now is just going to make it worse."

"Don't you worry about that fat ass Thomas. This is you and Anthony's life. Thomas is just gonna have to get over it. When are you going to tell Anthony?"

"Tonight, when he gets home from a party. Thomas is trying to smooth things over between the two of them."

"Let me know how it goes."

Randi was so excited that she could hardly contain herself. She was living a dream come true. She was in school for her writing, married to the best man in the world, and now she was about to have his baby.

She couldn't wait to tell him as she paced around the room and tried to come up with the words to tell her husband that they were expecting. She hoped that he would be as happy as she was. Overwhelmed with excitement, she couldn't wait another second and decided that she would go over to the party and tell him.

***

Anthony looked at his watch. It was 11:15. He wondered how Randi was feeling. He sipped his champagne and watched Thomas's lips as he tried to talk while holding his cigarette in his mouth. Anthony wasn't listening to him, and he wasn't feeling the party.

He interrupted Thomas. "Man, I'm gonna head on home. You know Randi's not feeling good."

"Naw, dawg. You can't leave yet. Just give her a call or something. We've got some serious stuff going on tonight."

"Naw. She's got an upset stomach. I feel bad for leaving her tonight."

"Maybe she's feeling better now. Go give her a call. She might decide to come on over and join us."

Reluctantly, Anthony agreed and walked down the hall to Thomas's study to use the telephone. He sat on the edge of the desk and dialed the number. While he waited for Randi to answer, a beautiful woman walked in. He looked over at her as she approached him. She was scantily dressed, and he felt like tossing some clothes her way. The answering machine picked up.

"Hey, baby, it's just me. Just wanted to see how you were feeling. I guess you've already gone to bed. I'll be home in a few minutes," he said. His eyes remained on the woman, who now stood boldly in front of him. She smiled seductively. He hung up the telephone.

Before he could say a word, she started. "Thomas wanted me to check up on you to see if you needed anything."

"No thanks." He picked up his glass.

She took it from him and drank the remaining

champagne.

"Anything." She raised an eyebrow.

Anthony smiled. He was flattered. His eyes traveled down to her breasts.

"Naw, I'm straight." Her silicone implants resembled two over-inflated balloons.

She moved closer and pressed her body against his. "That's what I'm hoping," she said. Her hands rested on his thighs.

He gently pushed her away and stood up. "I'm flattered, but I'm also a happily married man."

"That's fine. I won't tell if you don't." She pulled her dress up and revealed her black lace thong and two perfectly round, caramel cheeks.

Anthony told himself not to look but he did. *Damn,* he thought. *She's got a phat ass.*

"You like?" she asked. She could read his expression.

"I've got a sick wife at home. I need to check up on her," he said.

She pushed him back down on the desk and stood between his legs as she pressed herself against him again.

"She's asleep," she said. "Let's not wake her."

He became aroused. He hated that other women besides Randi still turned him on.

***

The drive was only thirty minutes, but it seemed like it took forever to get to Thomas's house. The driveway was filled with cars. This was some party, she thought as she got out of her car and went inside. The party reminded her of the one she went to when she met Anthony. Music blasted from the speakers and half-naked women gyrated to the beat.

She didn't see Anthony but spotted Thomas. Maybe Anthony was headed home. She wondered if they worked things out. She walked over to Thomas to ask if Anthony was still there.

***

"I gotta get out of here." Anthony told the woman as she slid her hand down to his crotch and grabbed his swollen manhood. She smiled at this.

"Damn, you must be happy to see me." She gently squeezed him, feeling the thickness. "Really happy," she added as she slid down his body until she was squatting in front of him. She unfastened his pants.

"Don't do that," he said, but he didn't try to stop her. *What in the fuck are you doing?* he asked himself. *Stop this bitch.* He didn't move.

She pulled out his swollen manhood and smiled up at him before she slipped it into her mouth.

"Shit," he said as he stood up to stop her.

She wouldn't stop. She slipped his pants down around his ankles and pushed him back against the desk. The things she did with her mouth were incredible.

He thought about Randi. He thought about how much this would hurt her, how much it would break her heart if she knew what he was doing. He tried to walk away, but his body wouldn't let him. He closed his eyes. *Nigga, you're fucking up,* he told himself. *You're fucking up.*

***

"Hey, Randi." Thomas smiled as she approached him. He seemed a little too friendly. After all, she knew he hated

178

her. "I thought you weren't feeling good."

"I wasn't, but I needed to see Anthony and it couldn't wait. Is he still here?"

"Yeah. He's in my study. He wanted to make a call. Go right down the hall and it's the second door on the left." He was all too eager to help her.

"Thanks." She headed in the direction he pointed.

Thomas was pleased. This was better than he had planned.

When Randi got to the door, it was closed. She knocked lightly then opened it. What she saw almost knocked her down. Anthony was leaning against a desk with his pants down around his ankles. A woman was down on her knees in front of him, giving him a blow-job. Anthony's eyes were closed until he heard the door open. He jumped up and looked at Randi like a deer caught in headlights.

Randi couldn't speak. She felt as if the room was spinning. She couldn't believe her eyes. This had to be a cruel joke. This couldn't be real.

The woman continued to give him head. Randi stumbled backwards, shaking her head. She was in a daze. Her body started screaming inside. How could he do this to her? This was her husband. This was the man she loved more than life itself. This was the father of her child.

"Randi!" Anthony broke the silence as he shoved the woman off him and onto the floor.

"You bastard!" the woman screamed as he struggled to pull up his pants.

Still dazed, Randi turned and bumped into the wall. She grabbed onto it to try to steady herself. Tears raced down her face as she felt her heart being crushed. She stumbled into the hall like a drunk and began to run.

Anthony chased after her, calling her name. He knew

he had really fucked up. The look on her face was indescribable. He had never seen it before, and never wanted to see it again.

Randi clumsily raced down the hall and back into the crowd of people as she tried to find her way out. Tears clouded her vision as she pushed her way through. She couldn't breathe. She felt like she was drowning as she gasped for air. She could still hear Anthony as he continued to call after her.

When she reached the front door, Thomas grabbed her arm. "Randi, are you all right?" he asked. Inside, he was thrilled. *Good old Anthony.* He hadn't let him down.

Embarrassed, Randi couldn't look at him. She pulled away and hurried out of the house. She ran to her Jaguar and fumbled with the keys before she could get the door unlocked. Once opened, she jumped in the car and locked it. Again, she struggled with the key as she tried to put it in the ignition.

Anthony raced up to her car and tried to open the door. "Randi! Open the door!" He beat on the window. "Open the door, baby!"

She finally managed to get the key in the ignition and started the car. Although tears clouded her vision, she sped off and left him standing in the driveway, screaming her name.

Anthony jumped in his car and chased after her. What in the hell was he thinking, jeopardizing his marriage for a blow-job? He couldn't get the look on her face out of his head. The look in her eyes reflected the pain that he had put in her heart. She was hurt and he was to blame. He was no better than Eric was.

***

She didn't know how she managed to get home

without getting herself killed, but she did. She ran up the stairs and into her bedroom where she started breaking things. She grabbed one of his gulf clubs and swung it like a baseball bat at everything she could see. She wanted to break everything he owned the same way he had broken her heart.

She went to the cabinet filled with all of his awards and started swinging. The glass shattered and his music awards fell to the floor. She knocked all of his gold and platinum records off the wall. Then she moved on to his cologne and the DVD system.

She trusted him, and this was how he repaid her. How many times had this happened? How many times did she sit at home waiting for him, missing him while he was off fucking someone else? She was a fool. Why did he do this to her? Why did he insist on ruining her life?

She swung the clubs at their wedding pictures, his PlayStation, the vase that held the flowers he sent her just because. He should have let her walk away from him when they first met. Why did she let herself fall for him?

Anthony heard the sound of breaking glass when he ran into the house. He raced up the stairs, taking them two at a time.

"Randi," he called as he entered the bedroom. She swung around to see him. He was nothing but a blurry vision to her.

Without thinking, she raised the golf club and swung at him. He dodged.

"Randi!" He tried to get the club from her and she swung at him again.

"I hate you!" she screamed. "How could you do this to me?"

"I'm sorry, baby. I swear this was the first and only time." He knew that he deserved an ass whipping.

181

She looked at him. Tears streamed down her face. Her breathing was ragged. He had no idea of what his infidelity had done to her.

He knew she was tiring, so he tried to take the club from her again. She swung at him with all her strength. He dodged and when she spun around, he grabbed her from behind. His arms wrapped around hers as he held them to her side. He wrestled the club from her and threw it against the wall.

"How could you?" she screamed through her tears. "How could you do this to me?" She struggled to get away from him. He held her tight.

"Baby, I'm sorry. I didn't mean for it to happen. I swear." He tried to explain.

"I hate you!" She was powerless against him as he held her captive in his arms. "Let me go!"

"Let me explain," he pleaded. "Let me tell you what happened."

"I know what happened!" The more she struggled, the tighter his grip became.

He pulled her down to the floor as he leaned up against the wall, never loosening his hold on her.

"While I'm at home waiting for you, you're running around fucking everybody!"

"No, Randi. This was the first and last time." He tried to explain. "I wasn't going to sleep with her. It was just a blow-job. And I didn't mean for it to happen."

"What happened? Did you trip and your dick fell in her mouth? You told me you fell into pussy every day. I guess you're falling into mouths too."

"I fucked up, Randi, but it never happened before. I swear this was the first time. I was trying to call you. Thomas sent her in there. I think he set me up, baby."

"So, he's the one that stuck your dick in her mouth."
Randi's body began to tire as she slowly stopped struggling.
"Oh God!" She cried out. "Oh God! Why did you do this to
me? You're supposed to love me. You promised me you
would never hurt me." She sobbed uncontrollably. "You
promised me, Anthony."

"I know, baby, but I fucked up. I fucked up bad. I
swear I fucked up," he repeated as he rocked her in his arms.
That was the only way he could describe it. He had fucked up.

Her body ached from crying. His tears streamed down
his face onto hers as they cried together. He was determined
not to let her go.

She couldn't get the image of this woman with her
husband out of her mind. Randi cried until she was exhausted.
Hours passed before she finally fell asleep.

Anthony didn't know how to fix it, but he knew he
couldn't lose Randi. She meant everything to him. He pushed
her hair back and looked down at her swollen, tear-stained
face. How could he have done this to her? He closed his eyes
and leaned his head against the wall. He knew that this could
very well be the end of his marriage.

Chapter 19

When Randi woke up the next morning, his arms were still wrapped around her but he was asleep. She thought about the night before. Maybe she had a nightmare. Maybe she hadn't caught her husband with another woman. When she looked around the room at all the damage she had caused, she knew it wasn't a dream, and all the pain came rushing back. She carefully slipped out of his arms, packed her bags and left him sitting on the floor, still asleep.

Anthony awoke to find Randi gone.

"Fuck," he said as he got up off the floor. He saw that her bags were gone. She left him. The only place that he knew she would go was to Kathy's. He called her and frantically paced the floor while he waited for her to answer the telephone.

"Hello?"

"Hey, Kathy. It's Anthony." He stopped pacing and tried to sound calm.

"Hey. I hear congratulations are in order." She sounded cheerful.

"Congratulations?" He thought she was being sarcastic. Randi must have told her everything. "What are you talking about?"

"The baby."

"Baby? What baby?" He was puzzled.

"Randi didn't tell you? I thought she told you." Kathy didn't understand why her best friend, who was ecstatic last night about being pregnant, hadn't told her husband the good news.

"Randi didn't tell me what?"

"She took a pregnancy test last night. It was positive. She thought she was pregnant. Maybe she's not. Maybe that's why she didn't tell you."

Anthony sat down on the edge of the bed and closed his eyes. It all fell into place—the upset stomach, the tiredness. That's why she came to the party last night. She came to tell him she was pregnant, that he was going to be a daddy. He had fucked up royally. He knew he was in jeopardy of losing his wife and his child.

"Have you talked to her today?" He had to find her.

"No. The last time I talked to her was last night. That's when she told me about the baby. Is anything wrong?"

"No," he lied. He looked around at the room. It was shattered like their world, he thought. He noticed their wedding pictures, lying in cracked frames all over the floor. "But if she calls you, could you call me and let me know?"

Now Kathy was worried. "Where is she, Anthony?"

"I don't know," he admitted. "She left me." He pushed his hand back through his hair.

"Why? What happened?" She knew her friend was in trouble.

"Could you just let me know if you hear from her?"

"Sure." She wouldn't push him.

"Thanks." He hung up the telephone and picked up one of the wedding photos. It was a picture of them kissing. He poured the shattered glass onto the floor and set the picture back on the nightstand. Where in the hell could she be?

Twelve hours later, Randi arrived at Kathy's house.

"What's wrong?" Kathy asked as she grabbed her and pulled her into the apartment.

Randi looked drugged. Her face was swollen from

crying. Her head ached. She didn't answer.

"Anthony called looking for you. He said you left him."

Randi didn't want to talk about it. She knew that if she did, she would start crying again. "I need to lie down," she finally muttered.

"Okay," Kathy said. She wanted to help her friend, but didn't know how.

Randi went into the bedroom and lay face down with her, head turned away from the door. She was dying inside, and she didn't know what to do to save herself. She didn't want to save herself. She just wanted to lay there and die.

Kathy came into the room a couple of times and tried to get her to eat or drink something, but Randi was unresponsive.

***

Anthony stormed into Thomas's office. He was busy with some other clients, but Thomas stood up at the sight of him. He knew that the shit had hit the fan. Thomas asked his other clients to give him a minute with Anthony.

"You set me up," was the first thing Anthony said.

"I don't know what you're talking about." Thomas played dumb.

"You sent that bitch in there to fuck with me and then you sent Randi to catch me." He paced the office, his nostrils flaring like a raging bull.

"Listen, Anthony," Thomas said calmly. "I may have set you up. Fact is, I sent the bait, but you're still the one who shoved your dick down her throat, not me. Randi showing up like that was something that I hadn't anticipated, but boy, it was perfect timing." He grinned.

Anthony stopped pacing and looked at his manager. "Why?" he asked. "Why would you do that?"

"Being in love isn't good for your career. You won't go on tour. You can't be away from home too long. You've lost your edge. You've become a lovesick idiot since you met that bitch." He reached for a cigarette.

Anthony snatched him up by the collar and shoved him against the wall. He pushed his fist into Thomas' windpipe.

"That woman that you're so quick to call a bitch is my wife, and she's carrying my child. If I don't get them both back, then you're a fucking dead man." He let him go.

Thomas crumpled to the floor, gasping for air, and Anthony walked out of his office.

***

Randi awoke to the sound of the telephone.

"Hello?" Kathy said.

"It's me again," Anthony said. "Have you heard from her yet?"

"Yeah, she's here."

"Thank God." He felt a wave of relief. "Is she all right?"

"She's just laying there in the bed. She won't even talk to me. What's wrong with her, Anthony?"

"Don't let her leave. I'll be there as soon as I can get a flight."

"I'll tell her."

"Thanks."

"Bye." She hung up the telephone then poked her head in the doorway to see if Randi was awake. "Randi," she whispered.

She didn't answer.

Kathy walked over to the bed and knelt down in front of her. "Baby, you're breaking my heart. Tell me what's wrong."

Randi just looked at her friend. She couldn't tell her. She felt like such a fool. How could she have let this happen? How could she have been so blind? Her eyes began to well up with tears. She turned her head so her friend couldn't see them.

Kathy rubbed Randi's back. "Anthony's on his way."

Randi rolled over onto her side, with her back against Kathy, and curled up into the fetal position. She cried silently as tears soaked her pillow.

Twelve hours later, Anthony knocked on Kathy's door. Randi could hear the voices. She wanted to get up and run, but her body betrayed her. She couldn't move.

"Hey," Kathy said to Anthony.

"Can I come in?" he asked.

"Sure. You look like shit."

"How's she doing?"

"Not good. She won't eat. She won't drink. She won't even talk to me. All she does is lay there and stare at the wall. Last night she cried for hours."

"You think she'll talk to me?"

"I don't know, but you can try. Maybe you can convince her to eat something. This starving herself can't be good for her or the baby." She looked at him hard as she tried to figure out what was wrong. She knew that he loved her, but he had fucked up somewhere along the line.

"Anthony, you didn't hit her, did you?" She remembered what Eric did to her friend, how he left her there to die.

"No," he said immediately. "I would never do that."

"Then you fucked around on her." She was afraid of what his answer would be.

He didn't say anything. He just stared at her.

She knew the answer. She closed her eyes and turned her head away from him. She had gone to bat for this guy. She was the one that kept pushing Randi to him when she wanted to run. She looked back at him. "How could you do some shit like that?"

"I know I fucked up, but it wasn't something that I planned."

She held her hand up to his face. "Forget it. You need to be talking to Randi."

"Where is she?"

"She's in the second room on the left."

Randi heard him walking down the hall. He poked his head into the room as if he was waving a white flag.

"Hey, baby," he said with hesitation.

Randi lay motionless and looked at him. The sight of him made her want to cry, but she refused to do so. She had cried enough over him. He wasn't worth another tear.

He cautiously entered the room and moved over to the bed where she lay. He knelt down beside her.

Kathy was right. He did look like shit. She hoped he felt like shit too.

He gently laid his hand on her stomach. She knew he knew about the baby. His thumb traveled gently back and forth across her belly. Two days earlier that would have turned her on, but now the thought of him touching her made her feel sick. How could he put his hands on her after what he did? How could she let him after what she saw?

She couldn't get the image of that woman giving him

head out of her mind. The way he stood there enjoying it made her angry. If she was a real woman, she would have beaten the hell out of both of them. Instead, she curled up and crawled away like a struck dog with her tail between her legs.

His thumb moving back and forth irritated her. She pushed his hand off her belly.

"I'm sorry" he apologized nervously. He looked down at the floor then back at her angry, pain-filled eyes.

She could tell he had been crying. His eyes were red and swollen.

"Kathy told me about the baby. I'm happy about it."

Randi silently stared at him. She hated him. She hated the sight of him. She hated the scent of him. She hated his presence.

"You need to eat." He was worried about her and the baby's health. "Kathy says that you're not eating but you need to."

She didn't respond.

"Randi, say something. Talk to me. Curse me out. Slap the shit out of me. Do something."

She still didn't respond.

"Baby, I love you and I'm sorry. That was the first time that happened. I've never cheated on you before. I swear." He tried to make his case. "I've got no excuses for what I did, but I was drinking and Thomas admitted to me that he set me up. You know he's been trying to break us up since we got married."

She knew Thomas didn't like them together, but that was no excuse to blame him for this. And if he did set Anthony up, that was still no excuse for him to stick his dick in this girl's mouth.

He continued. "I only went into his study to call you. I wanted to check up on you because I knew you were sick. I didn't even want to go to the party. I went to call you, but you didn't answer. I thought that maybe you had gone to bed so I just left a message. That woman came in afterwards. When she started coming on to me I tried to stop her."

Randi didn't want to hear this.

"I tried to stop her, but I didn't. I swear, baby, it just happened. I didn't go to the party expecting this."

Her eyes began to well up with tears. Although she tried to hold them back, she couldn't. She blinked, and the tears rolled down the sides of her face.

"I'm sorry, Randi. I swear it'll never happen again. I promise you, baby. And as soon as I can get out of my contract with Thomas, he's gone."

Even if he was telling the truth, Thomas hadn't undone his pants. Anthony still had the option to walk away from this woman, but he didn't. And what was worse was the fact that he enjoyed it.

"Randi, please say something."

She didn't. She just lay there like a rag doll. She slipped from being angry to being sad again. This was her husband. This was the man that she loved ridiculously. This was the father of her child. How could he have just given himself to a complete stranger? How could he have so much disregard for their love? Didn't he love her enough to say no, to just walk away? How many more times had this happened? How could she ever trust him again?

He finally sat down on the floor beside the bed with his back against the wall. He didn't know what to do, but he knew that he wasn't leaving there without her. To him, it didn't matter much that she wouldn't talk to him. Just being close to her again was good enough. They sat in silence for quite a while before he started talking again.

"Randi, we can make it through this. We've got a baby

on the way. We can do this." He looked over at her. She didn't move.

Kathy knocked on the door and stuck her head in. "How's it going?" she asked Anthony. She carried a tray of food. He looked up at her and shook his head.

"Well, I fixed her something to eat. Maybe you can get her to eat it." She placed the tray on the table next to him.

He stood up over Randi. "You need to eat, baby."

She didn't move.

He leaned over the bed and pulled her lifeless body up. After he propped her up against the headboard, he picked up the tray and sat on the bed in front of her.

"Are you going to eat?" He held out a spoon for her.

Kathy had fixed her some soup and crackers. Randi just looked at it. She didn't feel like eating. She didn't feel like living.

"You've got to eat something," he said, still holding the spoon out for her. She just sat there looking as if she had been drugged.

Determine to make her eat, he scooped up some soup with the spoon and attempted to feed it to her.

She slowly lifted one of her hands and reached for the spoon. He carefully gave it to her so she wouldn't spill it. She brought it to her mouth and sipped. Almost automatically she lowered the spoon back into the soup and brought it to her lips again. She couldn't taste it; she couldn't smell it; she couldn't even feel its wetness. She was numb.

Anthony smiled as he watched her. When she finished, she dropped the spoon into the bowl. He handed her a glass of ice water. She took a sip. He took the glass from her and set it back on the table. He was happy to see some life in her. She wrapped her arms around her knees as she drew them up to her chest and began to sway. He watched her as she gently rocked herself back and forth like a child. Her face was sad and lost. He could see what he had done to her, how he had drained the happiness from her body.

He reached out and touched her arm as if he was afraid he would break her. He already had.

"Randi." He gently squeezed her arm. She stared into his eyes. Had he lost her forever? "I need you to come home with me. Let me take care of you."

She only stared.

"I don't want to lose you," he continued. "I can't lose you and the baby."

She tried to see her husband. She tried to see the man she loved. All she could see was that woman giving him head. She looked away from him so he couldn't see her cry as the tears began to flow from her eyes. She rolled over and curled up like a baby with her back to him. This hurt so bad. When was it going to stop? She cried softly in her pillow.

Anthony climbed in the bed and curled up next to her. He put his arm around her waist and tucked his fingers under her. He held her like he had held her hundreds of times before, but this was different. This time he held her like he was afraid to let go.

Twenty minutes later, Randi jumped up from the bed and ran into the bathroom. Anthony followed. She leaned over the toilet and threw up. He held her hair back and helped her steady herself as her body heaved and spewed out everything she had eaten. He ran some cold water on a washcloth and helped her wash her face.

Anthony sat with Randi around the clock for the next two days. He held her when she cried, apologized to her every chance he got and tried to convince her to come home. It had been a one-sided conversation, but on this day, Randi finally spoke. She lay curled up on the bed and he stood by the

193

window looking out.

"Why?" she whispered.

Not sure if he was hearing things, he turned around and looked at her.

"Why was I not enough?" she asked. Her voice trembled.

He walked over to the bed and sat next to her. Staring into her eyes, he wished he could make it all go away, erase everything that had happened in the last few days. But he couldn't. He had fucked up, and he had to face the consequences.

"You're more than enough, Randi. You're everything."

She couldn't understand. "If you wanted oral sex, I could have . . . "

"It's not about oral sex."

She slowly sat up. "What am I doing wrong?"

"Nothing, baby." He looked up at the ceiling and tried to figure out why he let this happen. He looked at Randi, whose eyes searched his for an answer. "I was too cocky, and I let her get too close."

She didn't understand.

He continued. "When I'm out on tour, women are throwing themselves at me constantly."

She braced herself.

"They throw themselves at me constantly, but I resist them, all of them. I kept a safe distance and avoided letting myself get in situations that I may not be able to get out of. That's how I've been faithful to you. That night I did go into Thomas's study to call you. You weren't home. The girl came in and started hitting on me. Instead of getting away from the situation, I got cocky. I thought I could handle it. I figured that I'd enjoy a little attention from another woman and then I'd just walk away. I wouldn't have to touch her. She wouldn't have to touch me. I'd just let her flirt a little and then I'd walk away." He watched Randi's reaction to his explanation.

She had none.

"But she got too close. She started pushing up on me, rubbing on me, and by the time I realized that I couldn't handle what was going on, it was too late. I had let it go too far." He bit his bottom lip. "I got aroused. My head kept telling me to walk away, but my body wouldn't let me."

They both sat in silence. Randi closed her eyes and tears rolled down her cheeks.

"I'm sorry, baby," he whispered. He slid over to where she was and pulled her against him. Her head lay on his chest as she wept quietly.

Chapter 20

A couple more days passed before Anthony finally convinced Randi to come home with him. He promised her that he wouldn't bother her. He would move out of their bedroom, she could finish school, and he would be there to help with things for the baby.

Kathy took them to the airport. She knew that Anthony loved Randi, but she hated what he did to her. She held onto her friend when they were ready to board.

"You let me know if you need anything. You hear me?"

Randi nodded. Kathy looked at Anthony.

"Thanks," he said to her. He knew he wouldn't have been able to take his wife home if it weren't for her.

"You take care of her," Kathy said. "Don't let this shit happen again." She hugged him.

Randi didn't say a word on their trip home. He took her bags upstairs to their bedroom. The maid had everything cleaned up, and their wedding pictures were re-framed. No sign remained of the damage that Randi had caused.

After a couple of days, Randi decided to move back out. She couldn't handle the pain of seeing him every day. He tried to convince her to let him be the one to move out, but she wouldn't. He helped her get a place that wasn't too far away from him or her school. At least she was still in L.A.

She refused to take his calls, saying that she wanted to move on with her life, that he was no longer a part of it. Anthony was going crazy without her. He started a routine of sitting outside her apartment, watching her to make sure that she came home alone. He couldn't bear the thought of her being with another man.

One day while he watched her, he sat in his car with a half-full bottle of beer in his hand and two empty bottles in the floor. He looked down at the clock on his stereo system. It was 3:30 in the afternoon. Randi would be home any minute, he thought as he took a swallow of beer.

At 3:35, her Jag pulled into the parking lot. *Right on time,* he said to himself. He took another swallow of beer as he watched her get out of the car. She stood there as if she was waiting on something or someone. He hadn't noticed the Ford Explorer that followed her into the parking lot until a tall, dark, muscular brother got out. She smiled at him as he approached her.

Anthony sat up in his seat to get a better look as his wife talked to this man. They laughed, and she pointed up to her apartment building.

"Damn it, Randi," Anthony growled as he quickly threw his beer bottle down to the floor with the others and got out. He felt himself turning warm. Randi and the stranger started walking toward her building.

"Hey," Anthony yelled as he ran up to them. Randi recognized his voice. They stopped and turned around. She closed her eyes and shook her head when she saw him. She knew that he was going to cause a scene. She opened her eyes and looked up at him as he stood in front of them.

"What the hell's going on?" He stared down at her. His nostrils were flaring and he was breathing hard. She knew she didn't owe him an explanation, but she didn't want to make the situation any worse than it was.

"This is Mark Scales. He's in one of my classes."

"I don't give a shit who he is. What the hell is he doing here?" He was pissed.

Randi was surprised by the way he talked to her. She

had never seen him act like this before. He reminded her of Eric.

"Randi, is everything okay?" Mark finally spoke up. He looked up at Anthony and fixed his jaw as he set his mind for a street fight. He wasn't as tall as Anthony, but he would beat the hell out of him if he had to.

This set Anthony off. "What the fuck—" He growled as he looked down at Mark. "Is everything okay? Nigga, I'm her fucking husband and the father of the child that she's carrying. Hell yeah, everything is okay!" He turned his body as if he was preparing to take a swing at him. "You better get the hell outta here before I beat the shit outta you."

"Anthony!" Randi yelled as she grabbed his arm. "Stop it!"

He ignored her. She looked at Mark.

"I'm sorry," she apologized. "I'll bring it to class tomorrow and give it to you."

"You sure?" He looked concerned. He didn't like the idea of leaving her there with this raging mad man, even if it was her husband.

Anthony was losing his patience. He couldn't believe this guy. "Nigga . . . " He clenched his fists as well as his teeth. "You don't know who you fucking with!"

"Please." Randi touched Mark's arm.

He looked at her a while longer before he finally gave in. "Call me if you need anything," he said just to aggravate Anthony. He knew that she didn't have his number. He looked at Anthony without a word, shook his head and walked away.

"And you stay the hell away from my wife!" Anthony called after him then turned to Randi. "This is bullshit, Randi, and you know it. And you ain't fucking calling him either!" He glared at her as if he wanted to hit her.

She looked up at him in matched anger. She knew he

had been drinking because she could smell the alcohol on his breath. So this was her husband, she thought, the man that she was married to.

"Why are you doing this to me?" she asked. Her lips trembled.

He ignored her question. "What were you gonna do, fuck him just to get back at me?"

She couldn't believe what he was saying. It was all she could do not to reach up and slap him. Her breathing became hard as she fumed over his comment. "I'm going to ignore that remark because I know you're drunk."

"I'm not drunk. I'm just mad as hell. Now, what the fuck was he doing here?" he demanded.

"I'm not dealing with this." Randi breathed out as she turned to walk away.

"Oh, hell no." Anthony grabbed her arm and spun her back around to face him. "You're not walking away from me. You got some swollen-ass nigga over here and then—"

"No!" Randi cut him off. "I think you've got it backwards. I didn't do anything wrong, Anthony. You were the one who screwed up. You were the one who threw our marriage away for a blow-job. Now, let me tell you what isn't going to happen. I am not gonna stand here and let you verbally abuse me like one of your hos. Did you forget who I am? I'm your wife. I don't care how angry you are or how hurt you are or how drunk you are when you see me. You will talk to me like you've got the good sense that God gave you." She snatched her arm away from him. "Now, I've got better things to do than stand here and watch you have a temper tantrum."

Anthony stared down at her small, angry face as it turned red. It had been a while since she had to stand up to him. He had almost forgotten how spirited she could be. He had forgotten that she wasn't a pushover for him and that she would put him in his place if she needed to.

Although she was tiny, smiled all the time, and spoke softly, she was never one to take his bullshit. He may have had a few beers in him, but he still had the good sense to know that she wasn't going to put up with his crap. He decided that it would be best for him to back off. His entire disposition changed.

"I'm sorry, baby," he quickly apologized. "I didn't mean that shit. I'm just going crazy. I just don't know what to do."

Randi blinked. Tears raced down her face. She held her lips tight as she stared up at him for another second or two. Without a word, she turned and walked away.

"I just don't know what to do," he repeated as he watched her disappear into her building.

When Randi got inside her apartment, she quickly locked the door behind her, slid down onto the floor, pulled her knees to her chest and sobbed quietly. How was she ever going to make it through all this? How was she supposed to go on with her life?

Anthony stood in the parking lot looking up at her building. He knew that he had fucked up again, but he couldn't help himself. He couldn't let any other men come into the lives of his wife and unborn baby.

For the next few months, Anthony continued sitting outside her apartment building, watching her. He didn't know if Randi knew that she was being watched, but no more men followed her home.

He refused to work on his music and drank even more. His friends came over to try to cheer him up, but it was useless. Randi was his life, and without her he couldn't survive. He would just sit in a corner and stare at her photo while he attempted to drink his pain away.

He finally told his parents what happened. Sylvia tried to tell her son that it would be all right, but she could tell that he was slowly dying inside. His parents decided to visit him since they couldn't convince him to fly home for a while to get his mind off his problems. When they saw him, he was a wreck. He hadn't bathed or shaven in days, and he reeked of alcohol. Sylvia had never seen her son like this.

"I know you love Randi, but you can't let yourself fall apart like this," his mother said. "If you're going to get your wife back, then you've got to get yourself together."

"But she doesn't want me anymore."

"She caught you with another woman. She has to go through this. You can't expect to say I'm sorry and for her to just say okay. You know all the pain she went through before you. You just compounded that. Give her some time."

"It's been three months, Mom. How long do I have to go through this?"

"Stop being selfish," she snapped. She didn't like her son sounding pitiful, especially since he brought it on himself.

He looked at her with surprise. His mom had never talked to him like that.

"You talk about how long you have to go through this. What about Randi? That poor child is alone, pregnant, and heartbroken. You cheated on her; she didn't cheat on you. You'll go through it for as long as she needs you to."

He knew she was right. He made the mistake of spitting in the air. Now he had to wait for it to fall back in face. He didn't mean to be selfish, but he felt like he was drowning and he couldn't scream for help. Randi wasn't joking. This shit hurt, and it hurt like hell. Then he realized that if he felt this bad, he couldn't imagine what she was going through.

His mother's voice softened. "We've got something for the baby, so we're going to take it over to her. Meanwhile, you get yourself cleaned up and try to figure out what you need to do get this marriage back together."

***

Randi sat at her computer working on a story. Her doorbell rang. When she answered it, she found Sylvia and Paul standing there. She was surprised.

"Hey, baby." Sylvia tried to smile.

"Hi." Randi smiled, though she was puzzled.

"Can we come in?"

"Oh sure," she answered nervously. "I'm sorry."

They stepped into the spacious apartment. "How are you doing, Randi?" Sylvia asked

Randi took a deep breath. "Okay." Seeing them made her want to cry.

Sylvia could see this and she hugged her. It felt good to be held. Randi wiped a tear from her eye when Sylvia released her and then Paul hugged her.

"It's going to be okay, sweetness," he said before he let her go.

She invited them to sit down.

She was starting to show, and Sylvia noticed it. "You mind if I touch your belly?" she asked.

"No." She was the first person to ask. Sylvia put both hands on Randi's swollen belly and grinned with joy. She was going to be a grandma.

"I can remember when I carried those boys. Michael was quiet, didn't move around much, but that Anthony, he

202

was steady kicking trying to get out." They all laughed. "Do you know what it is?"

"Not yet." I'm having a sonogram next Friday. Then I'll find out." She was excited.

"What are you hoping for?"

"Doesn't matter. Just a happy, healthy baby."

"So, how's the morning sickness?"

"It finally went away. Thank goodness. I was so tired of being sick."

Sylvia was happy to see how healthy Randi looked. "You look like you been taking good care of yourself."

"I'm taking my prenatal vitamins and I try to eat healthy."

"And the doctor says everything with the baby is going well?" Paul asked.

"Yeah. He said my weight was good. My blood pressure was perfect. No signs of gestational diabetes, and the baby is growing at a normal rate."

"Anthony misses you a lot, dear," Sylvia said.

"I miss him too." She looked sad.

"But we aren't here to talk about Anthony. We've got something for the baby. It's in the car." She looked at her husband. "Could you go ahead and get it, dear?"

Paul stood up and went outside to the car.

"Is he doing okay?" Randi asked. "Anthony."

Sylvia smiled. "He's miserable. But he deserves it."

Randi smiled. She wondered if he was as miserable as she was.

Shortly, Paul returned, carrying the beginnings of a baby's crib. "I hope you haven't got one already," Sylvia said. "It's Anthony's old crib."

"No." Randi smiled. "I haven't done any shopping for the baby yet."

"If you want me to, I can go ahead and put this in the baby's room and set it up for you," Paul offered.

"You would do that for me?"

"Of course, sweetness. Just show me where the baby's room is."

She showed him to the baby's room then fixed them some refreshments. They all helped in putting the beautiful crib together.

"We couldn't keep Anthony in it," Sylvia said. "As soon as he could stand up, he was crawling out of the bed and climbing in the bed with Mike." They laughed.

"We have the rest of his baby furniture. Once you get the room painted we'll send it to you," Paul said.

"Thanks." Randi smiled. She was grateful that they didn't hate her for leaving their son.

Chapter 21

Randi sat in the waiting room at her gynecologist's office. She was scheduled to have a sonogram and she was excited. Since she was a little early for her appointment, she flipped through a baby magazine to occupy her time. She finished one magazine and reached for another. When she looked up, she saw Anthony walking toward her. She hadn't told him about the appointment, so she was surprised to see him.

A month had gone by since the incident at her apartment building. Surprisingly, it didn't hurt as much to see him as it did last time. He looked handsome, she thought as he sat down in the chair next to her. She waited for an explanation for why he was there.

He was nervous and didn't know what to say to her. She looked increasingly beautiful every day. Pregnancy agreed with her.

"You look great," he finally said to break the silence.

"Thank you." She looked down at the magazine.

"I'm sorry about the way I acted at your apartment," he said. "I was crazy. And that comment I made; I know you wouldn't do anything like that."

"What are you doing here?" Her voice was soft, almost a whisper, but she didn't acknowledge his apology.

He figured she was still pissed. "Mom told me about the sonogram," he said. "I wanted to be here. I would have called and asked, but I was afraid that you would try to talk me out of coming."

"I would have," she admitted.

She wanted to lay her head on his chest. She wanted him to tell her everything was going to be okay. She wanted to be able to believe him, but she knew she couldn't. "So, how are you doing?" she asked.

"Not good." It was hard for him to look at her and not be able to touch her. "How about you?"

"Not good."

"How's the baby?" He looked at her belly. He couldn't tell how big she was since she was sitting down.

"The baby's doing fine." She instinctively rubbed her stomach.

"Can I?" He wanted to feel his baby.

"Yes." She felt she owed him that much.

Gently, he placed his large hand over her small, swollen belly. He smiled as he felt the roundness of his baby. This was really happening, he thought. He was going to be a father.

This was the first time he had touched her in months, but it was still gentle and familiar to her. She looked down at his hand. He still wore his wedding band.

"Is she moving yet?" he asked with hand still on her belly.

"She?" Randi said. "You think it's a girl?"

"It is a girl. I can feel it." He looked in Randi's eyes. "Just like I can feel that you and I are supposed to be together. It's not too late for us, baby."

"Randi Talbert." The nurse called her name.

Randi looked over at her. "That's us," she said, avoided Anthony's eyes. She put her magazine down and they both stood up.

"How are you doing today?" the nursed asked when they reached her.

"Fine." Randi smiled.

They followed the nurse down the hall into the examination room. She instructed Randi to lay down on the table. Anthony set her purse down and helped her up on the table. He felt like they were a team again. He missed having her in his life so much.

"The doctor will be here in a minute," the nurse told them before she left.

Randi stared up at the ceiling while Anthony looked at the posters of the progression of pregnancy. He never thought about the whole process until he found out they were having a baby. Now he wanted to know everything about it. He looked at how the woman's body grew during each trimester. He was fascinated with how much the fetus changed as it matured, and he wondered what his baby looked like.

He glanced over at Randi as she lay looking at the ceiling. How could he fix this? She looked fragile, lonely. He was lonely too. He missed wrapping his arms around her at night while they slept. He missed listening to her light snoring when she was exhausted. He missed the way the soft skin of her legs felt against his when he rubbed up against her. Being without her made the days seem long and the nights even longer. Sleepless nights plagued him. He wondered if she ever rolled over in the middle of the night and reached for him like he reached for her.

Randi twiddled her fingers as she waited. Although it had only been three months, the picture of the woman with her husband had started to fade. It wasn't such a vivid memory anymore, but it was still there every day, reminding her how he betrayed her. Whenever she felt the urge to go back home, to tell her husband how much she still loved him and still ached for his touch in the middle of the night, the events of that night would come rushing back. She remembered how much pain he caused and she knew how much more he could

207

bring. Still, she missed the way he made love to her like she was the only woman in the world. She felt the love in his gentle touch and his soul-drinking kisses.

"Mom said that the baby's room needed painting. I can come over and do that for you." He didn't like the idea of her getting the baby's room ready. It was a sign that she wasn't coming back home. Nevertheless, if painting the baby's room was the only way he could get a chance to be near her, then he would do it.

She looked over at him. "You don't have to do that."

"I want to." He walked over to where she lay. "Please. Let me help."

She stared at him, not knowing what to say.

"I just want to help." He was desperate.

The doctor quietly knocked on the door and walked in with the nurse behind him. "Good morning, Randi." He wore a big smile.

"Morning." She smiled back. She liked Dr. Linville because he was personable.

"And you must be Mr. Randi," he said to Anthony. They shook hands.

"Yes, but you can call me Anthony."

He turned back to Randi. "How are we doing today?"

"Just fine."

"And baby?"

"Baby's fine."

"You feeling any movements, like fluttering?" He pulled up Randi's maternity top and exposed her belly.

Anthony smiled when he saw her fullness. That was his little girl she was carrying.

"Two days ago I started feeling the fluttering."

Dr. Linville pulled the stethoscope from around his neck and slipped the tips into his ears. He placed the chest piece on her belly as he listened for the heartbeat. When he heard the tiny thumping, he smiled and looked at Anthony. "You want to hear your baby's heartbeat?" he asked.

"Yes," Anthony quickly answered.

Randi watched Anthony's smile broaden when he heard his baby's heartbeat for the first time. She knew how he felt. It was overwhelming.

Anthony started to laugh at the quick little heartbeats that vibrated through his ears. He was happy to be there with his wife and his baby.

Dr. Linville measured Randi's uterus to see how the baby's growth was progressing. Everything looked like it was right on time.

"Are you ready to see what this little booger is?" Dr. Linville asked.

"My husband thinks it's a girl." *My husband*, Randi thought. It had been a long time since she said those words. It sounded good to her ears.

"A girl." The doctor looked at Anthony. "You know something we don't know?"

"I can feel it." He smiled.

"Well, let's see if your feeling is correct."

The nurse pulled the waistband of Randi's pants down even farther.

"This is cold," she told Randi as she placed tissue paper along Randi's waistband and prepared to spread gel on her belly.

Anthony watched as she squirted the greenish-colored gel all over Randi's stomach and smoothed it over with her gloved hand. The doctor pulled the ultrasound machine over to the table where Randi lay. She could hardly wait to see her baby.

The nurse turned on the machine. Dr. Linville sat

down on a stool by Randi's side and Anthony moved over and stood by her head. The doctor turned the monitor so they could see it. He placed the transducer on Randi's belly and moved it around as he tried to get an image on the screen. Randi and Anthony didn't know what they were looking at until Dr. Linville explained it to them.

"This is your baby's head," he said. "I'm going to take a few measurements." He clicked the computer mouse and measured from one side of the head to the other. "These measurements will help pinpoint exactly how old the baby is and when you should deliver."

Anthony stared at the image on the screen. He could see the head. He could see his baby. He was at a loss for words. Randi looked at the screen and then at her husband. The look on his face was something she wanted to remember. He was in total awe.

"Can you see it?" she asked him.

"Yes." He nodded without taking his eyes off the screen.

Randi looked back at the monitor as the doctor moved the transducer over her belly again. "Is that the arm?" she asked.

"Yes," the doctor answered as he took more measurements.

"I can see her." Anthony finally said. "She's beautiful."

The doctor measured the baby's legs and showed them its spine and heart. They saw it beating. It was unreal to both of them. They had created this miracle out of their love for each other.

Anthony looked down at Randi and his hand automatically stroked her hair. She looked up at him. She wanted to go back home with him. She wanted to be his wife again and raise this little baby together.

"So, you think you're having a little girl?" the doctor asked Anthony. "Are you ready to find out?"

Anthony and Randi looked back at the monitor.

"Yes," he said as he squeezed Randi's hand.

The doctor slid the transducer over her belly until both of the baby's legs appeared on the monitor.

"Well, she's not modest. Her legs are opened," he said.

"Her," Randi said. "So, it is a girl."

"It's a girl," Dr. Linville said. "Right here." He pointed to the area between the baby's leg. "If it was a boy, you would see the penis and testicles right here, but there are none." He looked up at Anthony. "You were right. You've got yourself a daughter."

Without thinking, Anthony leaned over and kissed Randi on the lips. Instinctively, she kissed him back. When he raised his head, he stared down at her. Randi avoided his eyes and looked back at the monitor.

The doctor printed out a few pictures of their baby and gave them to Anthony.

"Everything looks good. Baby's growth is consistent with how many months she is, so I guess we'll be having a baby in five months." He looked at Randi. "Have you signed up for your Lamaze classes yet?"

"No." She shook her head.

"The schedule is on the wall in the hallway. You can decide which times are best for you and sign up. Don't wait too late. Eight months is usually a good starting point."

She nodded. "Okay, doctor."

"Do you have any questions?" He looked at Randi then at Anthony.

"No," they said.

"Well, we'll see you next month," he said to Randi and

then to Anthony, "Nice meeting you." He shook his hand. "You take care her."

"I will," Anthony promised.

Dr. Linville left the examining room while the nurse gave Anthony some paper towels. "You can help her clean herself up," she said to him. "Randi, stop by the front desk on your way out so we can set up your next appointment."

Randi nodded and with that, the nurse left the room.

"I'm sorry about the kiss," he said as he wiped the gel off of her belly. "I didn't mean to. It was just . . . ."

"I know." She watched his face. Although he was more handsome than she remembered, she still saw traces of sleepless nights in his eyes. "Your mom says you haven't been working on your music."

He kept his eyes on her belly as he wiped the last few spots of the gel off her. "I can't think. Can't get you out of my head." He looked at her face. "I can't believe I threw away the best thing I ever had."

She pulled down her blouse and he helped her sit up. "You know you can't throw away your career over this."

"Without you, Randi, I see no point."

"It'll get better," she assured him. She knew from experience.

"Promise," he said.

"I promise." She smiled as she reached up and touched his cheek.

He put his hand over hers, turned his head, and kissed her palm. "I love you so much," he whispered. "Will you ever forgive me?"

She slowly pulled her hand away from him and slid down off the table. She picked up her purse, placed one hand on the doorknob, and looked up at him. "I forgave you a long time ago, baby," she said then opened the door.

Rap Superstar

He followed her down the hall and they stopped to look at the schedule for Lamaze classes. She found some class dates that she could fit into her routine.

"I'd like to be your coach," he said.

"It's only going to make it harder for you."

"I want to be there for you and the baby. I'm not gonna abandon you just because I screwed up. Whatever you need, I got you."

She agreed that he could be her Lamaze coach. After she set up her next appointment, he walked her to her car. She gave him one of the pictures of the sonogram and allowed him to touch his baby once more before she drove off.

It was hard to let her go. Randi promised him that it would get better, but he couldn't see that happening. He hurt just as much this day as he did when she first walked out of his life. He had to be patient. He had to get her back no matter how long it took. He knew she still loved him as much as he loved her. He just had to wait.

By the end of the week, he had gotten in touch with Randi. She agreed to go with him to purchase the paint for the baby's room. After they settled on a nice shade of pink, they returned to her apartment. He surveyed the apartment to see if there was any sign of him there, maybe a picture or something, but there was none. He was disappointed.

She showed him to the baby's room and told him what she wanted. He set up everything and started painting. After he put on the first coat, she fixed him some lunch. She sat down at the table and ate with him.

He listened as she told him about school and a novel that she was working on. She hoped to finish the novel before their daughter's birth. Although he was happy that she could

213

focus on her writing through all they were going through, he was disappointed that she seemed to be moving on with her life without him.

He watched her closely as he ate. The thought of divorce crept into his head. Randi had never brought it up, and he hoped that she wouldn't. He didn't think he could handle it if she did.

"Baby names." He took a sip of water. "Have you thought of any?"

"Yeah." She smiled. "What do you think of Sidney?"

"Sidney," he repeated to see how it would roll off his tongue. He smiled. "I like it. What about a middle name?"

"I'll let you have that one."

He had already picked a name. "Jordan," he said.

"Sidney Jordan," she said. She liked the sound of it.

"Sidney Jordan Talbert," he corrected.

"I can live with that." She smiled.

"I can too." He walked over to her, kneeled down beside her and placed his hand on her belly. "I love you, Sidney," he whispered then looked up at Randi. "Thank you for this gift," he said. "Thank you for this gift." He looked back down at her belly. "I'm gonna be the best father I can be, Sidney. I promise you that."

Later, when the first coat of paint dried, he applied a second. While he painted, Randi sat at her computer and worked on her novel. She leaned back in her chair and rubbed her belly as she tried to picture the scene she was about to start writing. She could hear Anthony singing. He sang Montell Jordan's "Missing You." It was one of her favorites. She whispered the lyrics along with him.

After he finished the room, he called her to look it over. She was very pleased. They sat around for another hour talking before he decided to leave. He didn't want to, but he didn't want to put too much pressure on her. It was as if they were starting all over again. He would have to earn her trust one more time.

Chapter 22

As the months went by, Randi and Anthony became more comfortable being with each other. They didn't talk about what happened between them. They didn't discuss getting back together. They became friends. He was there whenever she needed something; she was there to talk to him in the middle of the night when he couldn't sleep. He didn't think it was possible, but he fell in love with her even more deeply.

He watched as her body expanded with the growth of his child. She would let him feel the baby kick. It fascinated both of them. Randi couldn't get over the amazing feeling of her baby moving around inside of her, and Anthony couldn't get over how much more beautiful she grew with each passing day.

She watched how her husband's face lit up when they went baby shopping together. He was surprised at how small the clothes were, and couldn't believe that a baby could be so tiny. He was happy. She knew that in his heart he wanted things to work out between them, but she had resolved that it was over for them. She could be his friend again, but she couldn't go back to being his wife.

During her eighth month, she started her Lamaze class. Anthony was her coach. They sat on the floor at the class, Randi between his legs. The instructor told the mothers-to-be to lean back on their coaches and try to relax. Randi closed her eyes and leaned against him as he massaged her belly. It felt good to have his arms around her again. She felt safe. If only she could stay there forever, she thought, but she knew she couldn't. She knew that when class ended, they would go back to their separate lives.

Anthony listened intensely to the instructor as she assigned them exercises to perform. He wanted to get this right. He wanted to show her that he could be there for her, that she could trust him again, that it was all right to love him again. Randi had underestimated his love for her. They had separated over seven months ago and he was still there. He was still trying to fix what he had broken. Most men would have given up by then, but he hadn't.

She watched him as he talked to the instructor after class. He got some extra literature to read. She was impressed. He had changed. He wasn't the boy she met at Deveraux's so long ago. He was a man.

***

Randi's back had been aching for two hours and although she attempted to massage it to make it feel better, it was useless. She looked over at the glowing lights of her alarm clock. It was 3:09 in the morning. She sighed at the thought of her 8:00 class. She only had four more hours to get to sleep. She rolled over on her back and looked up at the ceiling. Her mind slipped to Anthony. She wondered what he was doing. Was he having another one of his sleepless nights, or had they finally left him alone?

She felt the baby kick. Sidney was awake. She placed her hand over her swollen belly to feel her kick against it.

"Hello, Sidney Jordan Talbert," she whispered. "What are you doing up this early in the morning? Can't sleep, huh? Me neither."

Only two more weeks, Randi thought as she rolled back over on her side. The pain was in her lower back. She tried massaging it again to no avail. It was a dull ache. It wasn't enough to call the doctor, but enough to aggravate her the rest of the night.

"Well, no need for us to lie here in the dark since we both can't sleep." She maneuvered her swollen belly around as she sat up on the edge of the bed. She slipped on her housecoat, went into the living room, and over to her computer. This would be the perfect time to work on her novel, she thought. With only a couple more chapters to write, she hoped to finish it before the baby arrived.

After turning on the computer, she wobbled into the kitchen to get a glass of water. In front of the refrigerator with the door open, she felt a lot of pressure on her lower belly. Soon after, a sudden gush of water raced down her legs. She looked down at the kitchen floor and found herself standing in a puddle. It took her a second or two to realize what had happened. Her water had broken. After the initial shock, she called Anthony.

Anthony rolled over and looked at the telephone when he heard it ring. He looked at the clock then back at the telephone. After just falling asleep, the telephone waking him up did not put him in a good mood. It better be an emergency, he thought as he picked up the receiver.

"Hello?" His voice was groggy.

"Anthony, it's me. It's time."

The sound of her voice woke him up fully. He sat up in the bed. "It's time," he repeated.

"It's time." She was calm.

He expected her to be screaming and hysterical. "But she's not due for another two weeks."

"My water broke."

"Your water broke."

"Stop repeating everything I say and get over here."

The pain in her lower back had traveled around to her

entire belly. She felt her stomach become rock hard as she had another contraction.

"Oh God," she moaned.

"Randi, are you okay?" He heard the pain in her voice. She didn't answer. She couldn't.

"Randi, what's going on?"

"Contraction," she said as the pain subsided.

"I'm on my way."

He pulled on his pants and T-shirt and hoped that everything was okay. She was two weeks early. First babies were usually late. He learned that from the literature he got at their Lamaze class. The baby's lungs may not be fully developed yet. He slipped on his shoes and ran out to his car as he prayed that they both would be all right.

Randi cracked the door so she wouldn't have to open it when he got there. She wobbled into the bathroom and put on a sanitary napkin, because with every contraction, a gush of fluid would rush down her legs. Between contractions, she worked. She pulled her packed suitcase into the living room, packed up some last minute toiletries, and called Dr. Linville. He said he would meet them at the hospital.

When she felt a contraction approaching, she braced herself for the pain. They came closer and closer together. She felt the pressure of the baby as it lowered itself down into her birth canal. Where was Anthony? She was afraid that she might give birth alone in her apartment.

The pain became so intense that the only way she could deal with it was to get down her hands and knees. As she watched each contraction pull her belly into a hard knot, she tried to remember her breathing technique.

"He-ha-he-ha-he-ha." She breathed. She assumed that

she was doing it wrong because it definitely did nothing for the pain.

When Anthony got there, he found her on her hands and knees. Thinking she had fallen, he ran over to her.

"Randi, are you okay?"

She looked up at him but couldn't speak. He tried to help her up, but she wouldn't let him.

"Contraction," she finally said when it was over. "I can handle them better from down here."

"Let's get you to the hospital." He helped her off the floor, grabbed her bags and they left.

***

"Oh God. Somebody help me!" she cried out as another contraction gripped her. She had been at the hospital for three hours. The contractions came, one on top of the other. Dr. Linville checked her cervix and she was only at six centimeters; she had four more to go. Randi didn't know if she could make it.

Anthony stood by her bed with a worried look on his face. He had never seen anyone in so much pain. She was drenched in sweat as the contractions assaulted her body. He tried to comfort her as he wiped the sweat from her forehead.

"It's going to be okay, baby," he assured her. "Just breathe like the doctor showed you."

"I don't wanna breathe," she whined. "It doesn't work. I wanna go home."

"I wish I could take you, but I can't." He tried to show her the bright side. "In a couple of hours we're gonna have a baby. We're gonna have a little girl."

She tried to smile. She knew he was right. This would all be over in a couple of hours and they would have a beautiful daughter to show for it. They would have a beautiful daughter created when their world was still perfect.

Another contraction charged her. She changed her mind. "I don't want to do this. I can't do this." She gripped his hand. "Please, Anthony. I can't do this." She moaned. "Please make it stop."

"Baby, I can't." He leaned over and kissed her. "I wish I could take the pain for you."

The contractions were so close that she didn't get any down time. She couldn't tell when one stopped and the other one started. She tried to adjust her body, but nothing she did relieved her.

Dr. Linville entered the room. "How are we doing?" He smiled, looking at the readout from the baby's heartbeat monitor. "These look pretty strong."

"She's not doing too good," Anthony said. "The contractions won't let up."

"Now, that's good news." He moved over to the bed where Randi battled another contraction.

"Is there anything you can give her? The epidural isn't working," Anthony asked.

Randi moaned in pain. "Please," she begged. "Please help me."

"From the amount of pain that she's in, it may be time to push. I'll check her cervix again, and then we'll work from there."

After checking her cervix, he informed them of the good news. "Well, you're one hundred percent effaced, the baby's head is at station minus two, and you're ten centimeters dilated, which in layman terms means it's time to push."

"It's time, baby," Anthony said.

She nodded.

"As soon as you get the next contraction, I want you to take a deep breath and push. And for every contraction after that, I want you to push like you're having a bowel movement, okay?" Dr. Linville directed.

She nodded again.

"Anthony, you help her by helping her sit up every time she starts pushing."

Randi felt the next contraction approaching. She took in a deep breath and pushed. Anthony started counting the way they taught him in class. "Seven, eight, nine, ten."

Nurses and doctors hurried in and around the room. Randi continued to push, but nothing appeared to happen. The contractions continued their assault and she became exhausted.

"This is hard." She moaned. "She won't come out."

"You can do it," Anthony encouraged her.

Dr. Linville sat between her opened legs. "Now, Anthony, with the next contraction I want you to help her sit up again and then pull her leg to her chest to help get this baby out."

Anthony and Randi both thought the doctor was crazy, and it showed on their faces.

"Follow the nurse's lead," he said.

The nurse stood on the other side of the bed. Without a word, Randi started pushing again. The nurse put her hand under the bottom of Randi's right thigh and pulled it to her chest. Anthony followed her lead by taking Randi's other leg and doing the same thing. Randi felt her bottom opening up.

"Five, six, seven, eight, nine and ten," Anthony counted. His face was so tense that it looked like he was the one in labor.

"That was a good one," the doctor said. "I can see the baby's head."

Randi wanted to laugh from relief.

"A few more good ones like that, and you'll be holding your little girl soon."

Randi pushed a couple more times using the same method.

"Okay, stop." the doctor said. "We've got her head."

Anthony leaned over to look as the doctor rotated the baby's head and cleaned out her mouth. He looked back at Randi.

"I can see her." He smiled joyfully. They were almost there.

"Now, give me one more big push then I can officially declare you Mommy and Daddy." The doctor chuckled.

Randi took in a deep breath and pushed with all her strength. She felt her baby pour out of her body and into the doctor's waiting hands. Her daughter started crying. It was a beautiful sound. Randi fell back exhausted into the bed. She was so happy that she started laughing and crying at the same time. Anthony rained kisses all over her face.

"You were wonderful." Tears of relief streamed down his face onto hers.

Without thinking, Randi looked up at him and whispered, "I love you."

"I love you too," he whispered back before kissing her the way she needed to be kissed. He savored the sweetness of her mouth as if he would never get another chance. She didn't try to stop him. She only wished that this could last forever.

Dr. Linville cleared his throat to get their attention. Anthony raised his head and looked at him. The doctor carefully handed his daughter to him.

"Hello, Sidney Jordan Talbert," Anthony said as he placed her across Randi's chest. "Meet your mommy." The baby continued to cry. She was beautiful and perfect.

"Hello, Sidney," Randi whispered. "It's nice to finally meet the little one that's been kicking my butt these last few months."

Sidney quieted at the sound of her mother's voice. She looked just like a doll baby. Giant, black satin curls covered her tiny head. She had deep brown saucer-shaped eyes that stared up at Randi. Her lips were full and bow-shaped like her father's, and she had round, fat, kissable cheeks. Her miniature hand wrapped around one of Randi's fingers. Randi fell in love with her immediately.

Anthony stroked Randi's hair and kissed her forehead as he stood by the bed and gazed at their daughter. He was in complete awe of this little girl. She was so tiny and fragile. She looked like she would break. This was his daughter. This was their daughter. This was his family. He looked at Randi. Through all that she had just been through, she was still the most beautiful woman he had ever seen. This was a day that he would never forget.

Chapter 23

A year later, Anthony rode through the streets of L.A in his new white diamond Cadillac Escalade. His head bobbed to the music that vibrated from his speakers. It was Sidney's first birthday, and Randi had thrown her a party. She invited her family and friends over to help celebrate.

A lot of things had changed in the past year. Anthony had started working on his music again after Thomas released him from his contract. Randi had graduated and published her first novel. Sales on her novel were so good that some executives were interested in turning it into a movie. Everything was looking up for both of them, but they still were not together.

On the day Sidney was born, Anthony decided to give Randi a year to come back to him. He knew that he would always love her and that she could never be replaced, but he knew that he couldn't wait for her forever.

He had no problem meeting other women, but he could never imagine loving anyone but Randi. He didn't want to love anyone but her. Although they didn't spend a great deal of time together anymore, he considered her his best friend.

He didn't know if she was seeing anybody new. They never discussed it, but he knew that one day she would. The thought of her with another man made his heart sink.

He did everything he possibly could to get her back, but she just couldn't get past his infidelity. He didn't hold it against her. He knew that if the situation were reversed, if he had caught another man going down on her, he would never be able to get over it or let it go. He remembered Mark Scales.

225

He remembered how he lost it when he saw him at Randi's apartment. The thought of her with someone else drove him crazy. No, he couldn't hold it against her for not coming back to him.

After today, the year would be up. He would have to move on. The thought of that saddened him. He wanted to be with his family, with his wife and his daughter. She just didn't want him anymore.

***

"Sidney Jordan Talbert!" Randi scolded when she walked into the room to find her daughter covered in chocolate cake and ice cream. She shoved another fistful of cake into her tiny mouth. Kathy stood in the living room laughing.

"Why didn't you stop her?" Randi asked.

"I was trying to feed her, but she wanted to do it herself." Kathy tried not to giggle.

"Let her be a baby," Randi's mother said, coming to Kathy's defense. "It's her birthday. Let her have fun."

"But Anthony will be here any minute and she's a mess."

"You do have soap and water in this big fancy house, don't you?" her mother teased.

Randi bought the house six months earlier. Anthony wasn't happy about it. He tried to talk her out of it, seeing it as confirmation that she was over him and she would never come home. Randi saw the house as a symbol of what she had accomplished. After all, her novel was doing great. She could afford it. Furthermore, she needed room for Sidney.

She wanted a place for Sidney to be able to run and play. Besides, her apartment didn't allow puppies and she had

226

purchased one for her daughter. Trouble was his name. Anthony didn't know it, but she named the puppy after him. He once told her that he couldn't avoid trouble; it always followed him around like a shadow.

"Stop giving her a hard time," her father, Randall, said to her mother. "You know how you were when the kids were younger. You wouldn't even let them play in the dirt."

"That was different," her mother said.

"Hold on, hold on. Let me tell you a story about when you were little." He shot a glance at her mother then continued. "When Randi was four, her mother wanted to wash her hair, but Randi wanted to play outside. So, when Sandra called her to come inside to get her hair washed, Randi ran. Sandra had to drag her into the house kicking and screaming. Well, she finally got Randi's hair washed, told Randi that that wasn't so bad, and sent her off to play." Her father looked at her. "You were so mad, Randi, that you ran back outside and threw handfuls of dirt into your hair." The whole room laughed.

Anthony turned onto Randi's street, pulled up in front of her house, and got out of the car. The sun shone brightly in the sky. Its heat felt good against his skin. *Nice day for a party,* he thought as he looked up at the sky. The forecast was calling for thunderstorms, but he could see no sign of any.

He noticed all the cars in the driveway. She had quite a few people there. The ones from out of town didn't just fly over for the birthday party. They also wanted to see Randi's new home. It wasn't a huge house, nothing like his mansion, but it was nice.

She was so excited about buying her first home. He remembered the first time she showed it to him. He was happy

227

for her but sad for himself. She wasn't coming home. *One year,* he had told himself then. *Don't give up yet. You still have six months to bring her home.* But today would be the end of his fight for her.

He looked down at his wedding ring and wondered if he would be able to take it off. Slowly, he walked up to the house and rang the doorbell.

Kathy answered it. "Hey." She smiled when she saw him. She gave him a big hug. She knew he was a good guy even though he had screwed up his marriage. She was just sorry that he and Randi couldn't get it back together.

"You look good," she told him.

"Well, I try." He laughed.

"Come on in." She moved back for him to enter.

He stepped inside and looked around the room. Although he didn't see Randi or Sidney, the rest of her family was there.

"Hey, everybody," he said as he raised his hand and gave a quick wave.

Randi's father stood up and shook his hand. "Hey Anthony. How you doing?"

"Just fine."

Randi's mother walked over and hugged him. Randi never told her family what happened between them to break up their marriage. They just knew that she was heartbroken and figured that he had been unfaithful. Still, they didn't hold any grudges against him. They knew that people make mistakes and they knew that he still loved Randi. He kissed her mother on the cheek.

"So, what's up?" Randi's brother, James, asked as he shook his hand.

"Nothing much. Just here to pick up Sidney."

"Oh, Randi's got her in the bathroom cleaning her up.

She got a little carried away with the ice cream and cake." He smiled. "Sit down."

"So, how's the music business?" her father asked.

"Just fine. Hip-hop is as hot as it can be right now. That's the place to be."

"Still making all the money?" James asked.

"I do all right." He laughed.

"Yeah, I wish I could do all right."

"You rap?"

"I can do a little something-something," he said, nodding his head.

Anthony pulled a business card out of his wallet. He gave it to her brother. "Give me a call sometime. Show me what you got. I'm into some new stuff now, and I need some talent."

James took the card. "Sure thing, man."

"Oh God," her mother said jokingly. "Not another rapper in the family."

Sadly, Anthony didn't feel like he was part of the family anymore.

Randi walked into the room carrying Sidney and her diaper bag. She smiled when she saw Anthony. He looked good as usual, but there was something different about him.

"Hi," she said as she walked over to him.

"Hey." He looked at Sidney. "Hey, sweetie." He smiled as he rubbed his hand through the giant black curls that covered her head. She started trying to jump out of Randi's arms when she saw him.

"She's ready for you." Randi laughed as she handed the baby to him.

He kissed her fat, juicy cheeks. She smelled like chocolate. She looked up at him with her big, brown, saucer-like eyes. She was beautiful, Anthony thought. She looked just like Randi.

"I put three changes of clothes in her bag, four bottles of milk and three jars of baby food. I only put in a few diapers since you already have some at your place. You think that'll be enough?"

"Plenty."

Randi kissed her daughter's cheek.

"Hey, Randi, can I speak with you outside for a minute?"

She looked up at him. "Sure." She followed him to the front door.

"It was good seeing you again," he said as he waved to her family.

"You too." They waved back.

He and Randi stepped outside the house. She closed the door behind them.

"Walk me to the car?" he asked. He looked serious.

"Sure."

"I read your book," he said as they walked side by side to the car. He looked over at her. "*Rap Superstar.*" He laughed.

"What did you think?" She was curious, since the story was about them.

"I thought it was great. I knew you were a great writer." They reached the car and stopped. He turned to face her. Sidney started pulling on his chin.

Anthony studied this beautiful woman. She was back to pre-pregnancy size. It was impossible for anyone to be able to tell that she had a baby. As soon as Sidney was born, she hit the gym hard, and within twelve weeks, she had lost all of the baby weight.

Anthony liked her determination, her drive to succeed at whatever she did. Too bad she didn't have the drive to make their marriage work. "You made me look like a good guy."

"No, I didn't. I made you look like yourself. You are a good guy." She smiled at him.

"So, is it gonna be a movie?"

"It's going to be a movie," she said excitedly.

"Congratulations. I'm proud of you. Everything that you wanted is falling into place."

"It is." She nodded.

"Well, I've made a few changes."

Sidney yawned. She was getting tired. She laid her head on her daddy's chest and tried to fight it, but her eyelids grew so heavy that she couldn't hold them open anymore. She finally submitted to sleep and began to snore lightly. Anthony smiled. It reminded him of Randi's snoring.

"What kind of changes?"

He leaned back against his Escalade. Randi stood directly in front of him.

"Thomas let me out of my contract, and I've stopped rapping. I've bought my own studio. I'm producing now."

She smiled. "That's good. I'm happy for you."

He continued. "I'm off the road. I'm home every night. I can be a full-time father. Most of all, I can be a full-time husband." He reached for her hand and pulled her closer. He looked down and saw she still wore her wedding ring.

Randi looked up at the sky when she felt a drop of rain fall on her. The forecast had called for it. She knew it was going to be a storm. She looked back at him.

"I still love you, Randi. I still need you. I want to be your husband again." Now he felt the rain falling from the sky.

Without a word, she pulled her hand away from him and took a few steps back. The rain started falling a little harder.

"You better get her out of the rain," she said then turned and started walking away. She wanted to be strong. She had been struggling with this for over a year now. She knew that she still loved Anthony and he knew it too, but to go back to him after what he had done was out of the question. Besides, she had just purchased a new home. How would that look to go back to him now?

Anthony sighed and closed his eyes. *Time's up*, he said to himself. He turned and started putting Sidney in her car seat.

Randi stopped and turned around. "Anthony," she called. She was tired of fighting her true feelings. She loved him so much that it was ridiculous. If going back to him was senseless, outrageous or just plain illogical, then she would be those things. She needed him. She wanted him, and she would be a fool for him.

He closed the car door and looked at her. She walked back toward him. The rain streamed down on both of them. He started walking toward her. When they reached each other, she looked up at him. Tears raced down her face, mingling with raindrops. They stood looking at each other without saying a word. He didn't know what to do. He brought one hand up and touched her face. "What?" he whispered.

"I still love you too," she whispered back. "I want to come home."

He couldn't believe his ears. "You want to come home?"

She nodded through her tears. "I want to come home."

These were the words that he had been waiting to hear for nearly two years. Without a sound, he lowered his head and captured her lips with his. Gently, tenderly, he savored her lips. They tasted sweeter than he remembered.

Her arms slipped around his waist as she pushed herself against him. Their kiss deepened as his tongue explored the depths of her soul. His hands slid down her neck and back as he crushed her against him. The rain pounded down on them, but they didn't care.

Anthony finally let her go. He stepped back and without taking his eyes off her, he opened the car door.

"Let's go home," he whispered.

She looked up at him and smiled. "Let's go home," she whispered back before slipping into the Escalade.

He closed the door behind her and looked up at the heavens. "I promise I'm going to get it right this time," he vowed before he ran to his side of the car and got in. He looked in the back seat at his sleeping daughter then at his wife. This time, he had to get it right. He had no more second chances.

Chapter 24

Two years later, Randi sat in front of her computer. She was working on her latest novel, *Platinum Princess.* Her back ached from sitting in the uncomfortable chair for so long. She tried to massage the pain away, but it was useless. Anthony constantly scolded her about sitting at her desk for so long. He had purchased her a laptop so she could write in bed, but she was stubborn and insisted on writing at her desk.

He walked up behind her, pulled her hair to the side, and kissed her neck. She closed her eyes at the touch of his soft lips against her skin. *She smells delicious,* he thought. It was her hair. It always smelled like a floral perfume. He slid one large hand down over her swollen belly.

She was eight months pregnant. The baby kicked against his hand as if it knew that he was there. It was a boy this time. They had already picked out a name for him. Randi wanted to name the baby after Anthony, but Anthony didn't want a junior. They finally settled on Nicholas Emanuel.

Anthony smiled at the thought of having a son. He had always wanted a daughter, but since he already had Sidney, the prospect of having a little boy made him feel good. His son could keep him company when Randi and Sidney were off doing girly things.

Randi anxiously awaited the arrival of their son. Soon after his birth, she would start film school. And while she was excited about having another baby, she didn't know how she would find time to juggle motherhood, school, and her writing.

Anthony was a big help. He would take Sidney to the studio with him to allow Randi some free time to write.

Rap Superstar

Sidney enjoyed going to the studio with her daddy. She liked the music and the people who came to see him. They were always nice to her, bringing her toys and candy.

After Randi converted *Rap Superstar* from a novel to a screenplay, they started filming. The movie was still in production. Marvin Sadler was handling everything.

Anthony was working with three new acts. He also produced the soundtrack for *Rap Superstar*. Randi's brother James had laid down a few tracks for him. Anthony was impressed and was interested in continuing to work with him.

Thomas finally came around and apologized to Randi and Anthony for what he did to them. Although they accepted his apology, they still kept their distance. They would run into each other at parties in the hip-hop industry and they were civil toward each other, but that was as far as it went.

Sidney was excited about having a little brother. She would rub her mother's stomach and call him Nick because she couldn't say Nicholas yet. She was fascinated by the way he kicked and moved inside her mommy's belly, and she had promised Randi that she would teach Nick how to rap after he was born. Dragging her keyboard and microphone behind her, she walked into the room where Anthony and Randi sat.

Anthony had given her the keyboard and microphone for Christmas. He wanted her to be a rapper. Randi wanted her to become an actress. They had plenty of years to go before they had to worry about her career, though she was growing up so fast.

"Daddy, look," Sidney said as she plopped down on the floor in front of her keyboard. She clicked on the power button and brought the microphone to her tiny lips. They both looked over at her.

Earlier, Randi had brushed Sidney's giant curls up into a ponytail on top of her head, but Sidney had taken it loose.

She always liked to play with her hair. This drove her mother crazy. Her once neat curls now spilled all over her head and almost covered her large, round eyes. Randi wondered how she could see what she was doing.

Sidney pounded on the keyboard and rapped into the microphone as her head bobbed up and down like her daddy's friends did in the studio. Anthony and Randi laughed. They could only understand a few words she said. The rest was unrecognizable.

They moved over to sit beside Sidney. Anthony helped Randi maneuver her swollen belly around as she sat down on the floor. He sat across from them.

"Let me show you how it's done," he said. "You play and I'll rap."

Sidney handed him the microphone as her eyes lit up. She loved to hear her daddy talk real fast to music.

Anthony leaned over and pushed Sidney's curls back away from her eyes. "Go ahead. Start the music."

She pounded on the keyboard but kept her eyes on him. Anthony bobbed his head up and down as he began to rap.

> *Mommy and Daddy and Sidney make three,*
> *In another month, we'll have another baby.*
> *Never in my life did I imagine this could be,*
> *My three babies make me so happy.*
> *And I'm never gonna give 'em up,*
> *Never give 'em up,*
> *Never gonna give up my family.*

Sidney giggled uncontrollably as she clapped her hands together. He leaned over and kissed her fat cheeks. She started pounding on her keyboard again. Anthony slipped his hand behind Randi's neck as he leaned over and softly kissed her lips. He had never been so happy in his life.

"Mommy, your turn," Sidney announced as she took the microphone from her father and handed it to Randi.

Randi laughed as she took it. She didn't know how to rap. Sidney started pounding away on the keyboard, her big brown eyes glued to her mother's face.

"Go ahead, Mommy." Anthony laughed. "Freestyle."

Randi laughed as she started bobbing her head up and down. She slid one hand over her swollen belly and rapped.

This little baby is kicking my butt,
This little baby has his foot in my gut.

Anthony threw his head back and laughed. "Heaven help us if you had to rap for a living."

"Hey." Randi pretended to be offended by the remark. "I'm a writer, not a rapper."

He slid over behind her and wrapped his long legs around her. She leaned back against his chest. He slipped his two large hands over her belly. She handed the microphone back to Sidney, who stood up and danced around, attempting to repeat what her mother had said.

This baby is kick my butt.
This baby is kick my butt.

Anthony watched his daughter as she pranced around the room. He lowered his lips to Randi's ear and whispered, "Promise me something."

"Yes."

"If I ever mention anything about her rapping again, you'll shut me up." He chuckled.

"Promise." Randi laughed. She had finally found her place in the world. There in her husband's arms, watching her beautiful, non-rapping daughter, and filled with the precious life of her son, she was happy.

Anthony smiled as he thought about how much he had changed in the past few years. Life was different now. Never in a million years did he think there was a life outside of rap. Never in a million years did he see himself right where he was today, married, with one child and one on the way. Never in a million years would he give this up.